"May I sit down?"
a male voice asked

Edie raised her eyes and stared hard.
She'd never seen a man with such
shattering good looks as the tall,
handsome one standing there. Her heart
pounded as she said reluctantly, "I'm
sorry. I'm waiting for someone."

"For me, I imagine," he drawled. "That's
if you are Alfreda Asher."

"Are you Drew Sutton?" She took a deep
breath, then flinched with the
realization that she had as good as
agreed to be his wife. She said nervously,
"Did you wait to see what I was like
first?"

"Oh, I'd have made myself known
whatever you looked like," he said
quizzically, and added with a kind of
quiet force, "we've made a bargain and
I'm sticking to it!"

OTHER
Harlequin Romances
by DOROTHY CORK

Many of these titles are available at your local bookseller
or through the Harlequin Reader Service.

For a free catalogue listing all available Harlequin Romances,
send your name and address to:

HARLEQUIN READER SERVICE,
M.P.O. Box 707, Niagara Falls, N.Y. 14302
Canadian address: Stratford, Ontario, Canada N5A 6W2

or use coupon at back of book.

Walkabout Wife

by

DOROTHY CORK

Harlequin Books

TORONTO · LONDON · NEW YORK · AMSTERDAM
SYDNEY · HAMBURG · PARIS

Original hardcover edition published 1979
by Mills & Boon Limited

ISBN 0-373-02288-3

Harlequin edition published October 1979

CHAPTER ONE

WHAT would he be like? Edie Asher wondered, look-ing bemusedly down from the aircraft to see its tiny shadow flitting like a bird across the spinifex-dotted plains below.

His name was Drew Sutton and he was a cattleman who wanted a wife, and that was virtually all she knew about him. Tall and lean and rangy was how she chose to imagine him, with a faraway look in his screwed-up eyes that came from gazing across the vast paddocks where his cattle roamed. He'd have a lazy drawling voice and he'd be fairly taciturn, so that she'd have to take the lead in the conversation. That he was a man of few words had been clearly indicated by the advertisement he'd put in the Sydney newspaper: Cattleman seeks wife, preferably under the age of thirty-five. A box number followed and that was all. Short and to the point.

'Exactly what you're looking for, Edie,' Barb had enthused. 'A man who wants to get married and no messing about! Why don't you grab your pen now and get in ahead of the rush?'

She hadn't seriously meant it, of course, but at odd intervals during that day, the idea popped in and out of Edie's mind. The fact was, she was absolutely sick and tired of men who *weren't* interested in marriage, and Joe's proposition the previous night had been just the final straw. It had been her day off and they'd been to dinner and then to a show, and when they came back to the flat she'd asked him in, because she liked him so much. Barb's door had been shut and her light was out, and soon Joe was kissing her and muttering things about wanting her and insisting, 'You don't have a lot of old-fashioned ideas about marriage, do you, Edie?' Edie did, and in a very old-fashioned way she started fighting for her virtue.

It had all been very wearying and very disillusioning, and she'd finally got rid of him by threatening to wake Barb.

In the morning, over their usual quick and easy breakfast in the kitchen, Barb had asked, 'How did it go last night, Edie? Was it a good evening? You're rather keen on Joe, aren't you?'

Edie gave a washed-out smile. Barb was older than she was, and worked as a biochemist at the hospital where she had done her nurse's training. 'Oh yes, it was a good evening—till he brought me home. I asked him in, but after he'd kissed me he wanted everything— right away! He's just the same as the others, and I won't go out with him again—not ever!'

Barb reached over for the instant coffee. 'Why ever not?' she asked imperturbably. 'I mean, men do have a habit of wanting everything, as you put it, once you've let them go so far. And anyhow, what sort of a man would he be if he *didn't* want everything, for goodness' sake? That way, at least you can be sure he's perfectly normal. Besides, I thought this time you were really in love.'

'Then I'm not any more,' Edie said shortly. 'I'm normal too and I want to get married. I didn't want the other sort of arrangement ... I'm sick of men,' she added after a moment. 'I'm twenty-two and I haven't had one single proposal of marriage. I really thought Joe was different—I really thought he wanted to marry me. But he doesn't—so we're *through*.'

'Oh, honestly, Edie!' Barb was a little impatient. 'Do you really mean to say that if he'd asked you to marry him last night you'd have been all starry-eyed and in love this morning—yakking away about bridesmaids, and asking him down to Wollongong to meet your sister? And contemplating sleeping with him after a certain date with perfect equanimity? But because the poor guy just wanted to make love to you, you don't even like him any more! That's really kinky!'

'I don't think it is,' Edie argued. 'It's just turned out we want totally different things. He—he *acted* as though he wanted what I did—before——'

'Well, of course he did,' Barb said with weary cynicism. She finished her coffee and when she'd set down her cup she picked up the morning paper. 'You know what, Edie?' she said, widening her blue eyes mockingly. 'The only way you can be absolutely sure a man means marriage is to answer one of those ads in the personal column. The ones that end "View mat.". *That's* what you should do, if mat. is what you so desperately want. Frankly, it doesn't appeal to me all that much—having to think up something to cook for my beloved's dinner every night, being stuck with his likes and his dislikes and his moods, and having to make my life subordinate to his. I'd settle for the looser arrangement any day ... Anyhow, let's see——'

That was when she found the cattleman's advertisement and read it out triumphantly. 'Just what the doctor ordered, Edie—marriage pure and simple!'

But while it had all been no more than a joke as far as she was concerned, Edie had answered the ad early that afternoon while old Mrs Hill, whom she was 'specialling', was dozing. Partly because the morning paper was there and she'd picked it up and unconsciously turned to the personal column.

A cattleman who wanted a wife! How romantic it sounded! And marriage—that was just her cup of tea. No informal arrangement that was betwixt and between, but *marriage*. Wedding bells. A whole future together.

'Dear sir,' she wrote on a page of Mrs Hill's notepaper, 'I am writing in answer to your advertisement for a wife, which appeared in this morning's paper. I am Australian born, nearly twenty-three years old, and a trained nurse. I am at present doing private nursing, mainly elderly people. I have dark hair and brown eyes, and am five feet four inches tall. I am fairly practical, as a nurse has to be, but I enjoy music and reading, and also tennis and swimming. I have no family but one sister, but I have a little money of my own left me by my grandmother who died four years ago. As well, I have managed to save some of my salary since I have been working.

'My present patient will be going to stay with her daughter at the end of this week, and since I have no further commitments just now, I shall be free to see you at any time after that, if you are interested in my application. Looking forward to hearing from you, I am yours sincerely, Alfreda Asher.' No one had ever called her Alfreda except her grandmother, but it sounded more dignified than Edie, more—serious, she decided.

She posted the letter on her way home that evening, and when she admitted a little exuberantly what she had done, Barb stared at her unbelievingly.

'Edie, you didn't! You're out of your mind!'

'But why shouldn't I?' Edie said recklessly. 'I mean,

he—he's a cattleman, and he wants a wife—a real
wife——'

'A cattleman! Is that what's gone to your head? He's
probably some old farmer who runs a few cows in
Woop Woop. All he wants is someone to do the milk-
ing and look after him and butter him up. If he turned
up on the doorstep here you'd probably shriek Yuk!
and dash for the telephone to beg Joe to come back.'

'Well, enquiring can do no harm,' said Edie, a trifle
dashed.

But he didn't appear on the doorstep. Instead, an
answer to her letter came remarkably quickly from an
address in Queensland—Dhoora Dhoora, via Narrunga, which didn't mean a thing to Edie. There were
no personal details, not even his age, to Edie's dis-
appointment. A brief and businesslike letter thanked
'Alfreda' for her reply to his advertisement, and continued, 'I enclose a flight ticket to Townsville and a
further booking that will bring you to Narrunga, where
you will be met. As you mentioned you had no commitments, I take it you will be free to travel on the date
for which I have booked your seats. I am also enclos-
ing a cheque so that you may do any shopping you
want before leaving Sydney.' He signed himself Drew
Sutton.

Edie read the letter twice, more than a little taken
aback. It was such an impersonal letter, and the flight
tickets were somehow so positive. As for the cheque—
crossed and made out to Alfreda Asher—it was for
five hundred dollars.

Barb was amused. 'You've scored a bull's eye, Edie!
What on earth did you say in your letter? Or did you
enclose a photograph? That way, you couldn't help
but win. Your farmer would think all his birthdays
had come at once!'

Edie blushed uncomfortably. She hardly knew what attitude to take now. 'I—I didn't send a photograph. And I didn't say anything much ... But this cheque—why do you think he sent it? I mean, what would I want to buy?'

'Can't you guess? Your wedding dress, dear—your trousseau. It's perfectly plain! You've been selected—you're going to be married at last.' She looked at Edie wryly. 'He's probably just like I said, you know—hayseeds sticking out of his hair and obviously an absolute fool, to send off five hundred dollars to a stranger just like that! What's to stop you going out and spending it and chucking those air tickets into the waste bin?'

'Nothing, I suppose,' Edie admitted. 'Only I wouldn't, of course.' Her own mental image of Drew Sutton was very different from Barb's, and privately she thought there was something rather distinguished, and very masculine, about his handwriting. Was he a fool? Or had he decided from her letter that she was trustworthy, genuine?—as she was.

'What will you do?' Barb asked. 'It's a bit of a giggle, isn't it? It would be fun to go and find out what he's like. You've got nothing to lose except your virtue, and my guess is he's not the sort to attack that very ferociously.'

Edie was only half listening. 'I'll have to go,' she said slowly. 'It wouldn't be fair not to when he's gone to all this trouble. But somehow—I didn't really expect to—to hear from him.'

In a way, she'd been caught out romancing, and now her fantasy was turning into reality, and she wasn't at all sure how it was going to end. One thing was certain, however, and that was that she would go to Narrunga and meet Drew Sutton. Not to do so, as well as being dishonest, would be like knocking on a door

and running away before it was opened, and she told
Barb with a touch of defiance, 'Arranged marriages
can work, you know—often better than the other kind.
My grandmother grew up in Ireland, and she used to
tell me and my sister how they'd arrange marriages in
the villages there. There were these big families, and to
get a daughter married, the father would have to see
she had a pig or something as a dowry to persuade the
boy's parents to accept her as their daughter-in-law.'

Barb raised her eyes to heaven. 'Good God, Edie,
what's that to do with it? You don't need a pig on a
string to persuade some man to marry you. I didn't
know you had one, anyhow. And for heaven's sake don't
go and marry the guy just because he's too hopeless to
be able to find himself a girl-friend by the usual
methods. If he tries to strong-arm you into it just
harden your heart and say goodbye and thanks, but
you've changed your mind, and come back home. It'll
cost you your return fare, that's all. Rather ominous,
that, the way he's sent you one-way tickets.'

Perhaps it was ominous, but Edie didn't really have a
great deal of time to think about it. She did a little
shopping, but she used her own money. She had always
loved fashion so she wasn't short of good clothes, and
while she most certainly wasn't going to buy a wedding
dress, she might well need a couple of pairs of jeans
and some casual shirts if she was going outback.

'Don't take too much gear with you,' Barb warned.
'If you turn up looking as if you've brought all your
worldly goods you'll have a hard time convincing him
you've just come to look.'

But despite her scepticism, Barb, like a good friend,
managed to take a couple of hours off from work to
drive Edie to the airport.

'Don't forget—you haven't burned a single bridge,

Edie,' she said before they parted. 'Your room's still here and I shan't even think about looking for a new flatmate. I'll expect you back ...'

That had been only this morning. Now it was late afternoon, and in the plane, Edie glanced at her watch and felt her pulses quicken. In not many more minutes they were due to touch down at Narrunga. Drew Sutton would be there to meet her, and she was going to have to face up to the reality of the situation. Quite suddenly, she knew that she couldn't marry a stranger —not possibly. Suppose he was like Barb insisted—oh dear, she was going to feel sorry for him! And really, you couldn't judge people by their appearance. Joe, for instance—he was really good-looking, and the minute she'd met him, which had been when he came to visit his grandfather whom she was nursing, she'd fallen for him. But look how he'd turned out! All he'd really wanted from her was sex, and the fact he'd bided his time before making that clear didn't make it any better in her eyes. In fact, it made it worse, because he'd won her trust by then. Maybe she was hopelessly out of date, and men didn't realise it because she didn't look that way.

She opened her handbag and taking out her mirror peered anxiously into it. What would Drew Sutton think of her when they met? Perhaps he'd think she wore too much make-up. He wouldn't be used to city girls. She examined her face carefully. In the brilliant sunlight—in the open air—would the soft grey-blue eye-shadow that enhanced the brown of her darkly lashed eyes look too artificial? And the luscious lipstick she'd been wearing lately as a change from the natural look—how was that going to grab him? In the outback, away from the glamour of city lights, was it going to look cheap? But right now the sun was going down and all that gorgeous golden colour that was streaming through the heavens was terrific for enhancing the light tan of her skin and the vividness of her make-up. Her hair was long and thick and dark and inclined to be curly, and she liked best to wear it loose, but today she had taken it back in one heavy braid that hung down her back. She wore a tomato-red sleeveless dress and a string-coloured cotton jacket, and high-heeled sandals to match.

'Will I be a shock to him?' she wondered as she put her mirror away and discovered that the plane was coming down. Isolated on the great sweep of the plains below she could see a small town of scattered houses, and beyond, a landing strip that looked fiery red in the sunset light. A few cars glittered in the sun. One of them would be his. She pictured him looking up at the plane, wondering what she'd be like. Wondering if she'd like him.

Oh heavens! The enormity of what she was doing struck her anew, and she felt terribly guilty, terribly sorry for this taciturn cattleman who had advertised for a wife. As well, she felt almost sick with nervousness. She probably wasn't in the least as he imagined, and—if he didn't like the look of her, if *he* was the one who said, 'Thank you for coming, but I've changed my mind'—wouldn't she, honestly, be immensely relieved?

Oh well, nothing was going to happen in a hurry. He wasn't going to grab her by the arm and hurry her off to church. He was just as human as she was. He'd want to get to know her before doing anything drastic ...

A few minutes later the plane had landed, and presently Edie was looking around for her cattleman. She started guiltily when a middle-aged man in white shirt and dark trousers spoke to her.

'Excuse me—would you be Miss Asher?'

'Yes.' Edie's eyes flew to his face and she felt the colour flood her cheeks. He was fifty or more—short, with a very Australian voice and a bulging figure that proclaimed him a heavy beer drinker. She felt her heart sink abysmally, but before she could force a smile and ask if he were Mr Sutton, he said, 'I'll get your luggage. How many bags?'

'Two,' she said, quaking. 'Are you——'

'I'm the taxi driver, miss. You're for the hotel, I've been told.'

'Oh yes—yes, that's right.' Edie did an instant mental adjustment and discovered that now she could smile at him quite happily. The taxi driver! Thank heavens! She waited till he'd got her luggage, and as she walked with him across to the taxi she longed to ask who had arranged for him to meet her. But she knew, of course, and she held her tongue.

Narrunga proved to be a small town, and there was a strong smell of sulphur in the air, from the artesian water, she discovered later. The hotel was a reasonably modern-looking one-storied building, and a few fan-shaped travellers' palms made patterns on its white walls, that were just now flushed to gold by the richly coloured evening light.

The taxi driver carried Edie's bags into the coolness of the lobby and when she asked him, 'How much do I owe you?' he told her with a friendly grin, 'You're all right, miss—it's all been settled.'

A room had been booked for her, she discovered at the reception desk. She signed the register and was given a key and told which way to go, but she had to carry her own bags.

'Now what?' she thought, frustrated and mystified, as she dropped her two bags on the floor and closed the door behind her. She looked around her quickly. Her room was largish, simply and coolly furnished, and equipped with its own small bathroom. The window looked away from the street into a dusty garden where the pink and white of oleanders mingled with the more flamboyant colours of cascading bougainvillea. Tired after the long day of travelling, Edie moved to survey herself rather dejectedly in the mirror. Her brown eyes were shadowed and her mouth drooped, and altogether she didn't live up to the gaiety of her red dress. She grimaced at herself, remembering how minutely she had examined her face in the mirror not very long ago. For what? To be met by an impersonal taxi driver and brought to this hotel. It was all a bit of an anti-climax. What on earth was she supposed to do next? Find her own way to Dhoora Dhoora cattle station? She'd fully expected Drew Sutton to meet her, but perhaps he was as shy and gauche as Barb predicted and hadn't been able to screw up the courage to meet her. With a sigh of frustration, Edie went into the bathroom to freshen up.

When she emerged, she rang through to reception, using the telephone on the bedside table, hoping not very optimistically that a message might have come for her.

Much to her surprise, there was a message.

'Oh, sorry, love,' the girl said laconically. 'It slipped my mind—there's a letter waiting here for you. You can come along and get it whenever you like.'

Feeling braced, but also apprehensive in case Drew Sutton had had second thoughts and left her stranded, Edie hurried along to get her letter, which she read standing in the lobby, aware that already the light had almost gone from the sky. Her eyes skimmed down the small half page of a handwriting that was familiar, though just now, to her rather jaundiced eye, it didn't look nearly so reassuring as it seemed to have looked before. 'Dear Alfreda,' she read, 'I hope you had a comfortable journey and that the taxi was on time. I shall not be in Narrunga until after you arrive, unfortunately. However, that should give you time to get your breath and tidy yourself up before we meet. I suggest the hotel dining room at seven-thirty. We can talk things over while we eat. Till then—Drew Sutton.'

Suddenly excitement sprang up in her again. In half an hour she'd be meeting him. And this letter—she read it again with intense concentration as if it might give up the secrets of the writer to her. Brief and to the point again—no romantic messages or suggestions about getting to know each other before they made any decisions. They were to talk things over. No one would guess that the final object of their meeting was, in fact, marriage.

Edie folded the letter away and slipped it in her handbag, then after a momentary hesitation made her way back to her room. If she stepped on it, she'd have time for a shower before seven-thirty, and most certainly she was going to change her clothes. Her dress didn't look nearly so fresh as it had when she'd put it on this morning.

As she stood under the hot shower, she reflected that at least it had been considerate of Drew Sutton to give her time to tidy up and catch her breath before having to face him. He couldn't be a recluse if he understood women as well as that. Why on earth did he have to advertise to get himself a wife, then? Well, soon she would know it all.

Determined for some vague reason to look her best,

she chose a powder blue dress of Swiss cotton. Carefully packed with tissue, it didn't show a crease, and it was a nice compromise between evening and day wear. It had a tucked hemline and its camisole top and narrow straps made the most of her smooth shoulders. She left her dark hair loose, and fastened small heart-shaped silver earrings in her ears and clipped a silver bracelet on her wrist. High-heeled silvery blue shoes completed her outfit.

In the doorway of the hotel dining room she paused. It was not a large room and not many of the tables were occupied, and she looked about her warily, trying to spot the cattleman, but she couldn't see a man among the half dozen or so there remotely likely to be Drew Sutton. There was only one man sitting alone—fat, red-faced, and when he looked in her direction he gave no sign that he was waiting for anyone. Thank heavens for that, Edie breathed inwardly, as she allowed the waitress to show her to a table and hand her the menu.

She was feeling annoyed again by now. It was pretty mean and thoughtless to keep her on edge like this. He didn't understand women after all. The thought entered her head that the whole thing might turn out to be a great big hoax, and for a moment she wanted to get up and run. But at five hundred dollars plus the cost of those air tickets from Sydney, it would be quite an expensive hoax ...

Telling the waitress with a pleasant smile that she wasn't ready to order yet, Edie decided to give him a quarter of an hour to put in an appearance, and if he hadn't turned up by then, she'd walk out and he could go to the devil.

'May I sit down here?' a masculine voice said into her thoughts, and Edie raised her eyes to find a tall, lean, and stunningly handsome man looking down at her. She stared hard. A tanned face, a thick wave of smoky brown hair over an intelligent forehead, silvery grey eyes that looked like chips of ice against the dark warmth of his skin, teeth that showed fantastically white in a smile that shook her—— He wore a satin striped shirt that had the merest hint of pink in it, a black tie and black trousers.

Wow! She had to be dreaming! She'd never seen a real live man with such shattering good looks, and her heart pounded madly as she told him reluctantly, 'I'm sorry, I'm waiting for someone.'

'For me, I imagine,' he drawled. 'That's if you're Alfreda Asher. I can't see anyone else who could possibly be she, and as it's'—he consulted the gold watch on his suntanned wrist—'seven forty-one, I took a chance on you.'

Edie took a deep breath, swallowed and said weakly, sure now that she must be dreaming, 'Are you—Drew Sutton?'

'That's right,' he confirmed, and sat down opposite her, leaning forward slightly to look at her with concentrated intensity. Edie leaned back, and tried to recover from shock. Barb simply wasn't going to believe this. A man like someone you dreamed about!—not a hayseed in sight. She looked up and met his eyes and flinched as the realisation struck her that she had as good as contracted to be his wife. Oh God! What was she thinking of? Suddenly she was appalled right through to the centre of her soul.

She said nervily, 'I—I thought you'd be here before me. Or did you—did you want to see what I was like first?'

'Oh, I'd have made myself known whatever you looked like,' he said quizzically, and his voice wasn't the slow drawling countrified one she had given him in her imagination. Nor were his eyes those screwed-up ones with a faraway look in them as he stared out at a mob of cattle in the hazy sunlit distance. They were fixed very decidedly on Edie Asher, right here in this small hotel dining room in Narrunga, western Queensland. 'We've made a contract and I'm sticking to it,' he added with a kind of quiet force.

Edie flinched again. He sounded so terribly definite. It wouldn't be nearly as easy as Barb had suggested to say goodbye and thank you, but I've changed my mind. And anyhow, the mad thought came into her head, why should she want to do that—now?

'You're—you're not like I expected,' she said jerkily.

'You're not like I expected either,' he reciprocated. 'I hadn't envisaged a nurse looking quite—like—you—look. Are you in fact a nurse?' he added, his eyes exploring the curve of her mouth—her shoulders.

'Of course I am,' she said, flushing. 'One doesn't have to look like Florence Nightingale to be a nurse these days, Mr Sutton.'

'One doesn't have to talk like someone out of a Jane Austen novel either,' he quipped. 'My name's Drew—and it's not short for Andrew. No one calls me Mr Sutton, Alfreda. Particularly not any girl I'm about to marry.'

Edie felt herself blush crimson. There it was again —like a statement of unchangeable fact. *Was* he about to marry her? Hadn't he better check with her first? But instead of taking him up on that point she heard herself say pertly, 'No one calls me Alfreda either, as a matter of fact. Not since my grandmother died.'

'No? Then what are you called?'

'Edie,' she said flatly.

He leaned forward and took the menu from her and she realised that her hands were shaking.

'You'll have to forgive me, but you signed yourself Alfreda and I've been thinking of you that way. Though let's face it, you don't look like Alfreda Asher ... Now what would you like to eat? I'd recommend the fillet steak with a salad, but you're entitled to make your own choice if you'd rather.'

'I'll have the steak, please,' she said quickly.

'It's a good way to get to know someone—over a meal,' he resumed, when he had given the waitress their order and asked as well for two dry sherries. Did he mean, she wondered, a little dazedly, that they'd get to know one another well enough over dinner to—to get married? There was a tenseness in the pit of her stomach that was definitely not due to hunger, and she recalled how she'd thought he'd be so quiet, that she'd have to take the lead in the conversation. And here she was struck dumb, while he was quite at his ease, leaning back in his chair and looking at her. Yes, he was still doing that, and she wished she knew what was going on in his mind. Glancing at him from under her lashes, she simply couldn't believe he'd advertised for a wife. Why, there must be a whole queue of girls who'd be ready to say yes if he asked them. Instead, he'd made an open proposal and chosen her, Edie Asher, for no reason at all that she could possibly imagine.

'Why did you choose *me*?' she asked abruptly, out of her thoughts.

He shrugged his broad shoulders. 'I calculated you'd suit me best ... What made you write, anyhow?' Their sherries had come and he raised his glass and looked at her across it.

'Oh, I'm sick and tired of men who aren't interested in marriage, I suppose,' she said uncomfortably, and saw a flicker of cynicism in his remarkable silver grey eyes that looked so vitally alive in his dark face.

'And you *are* interested. For any particular reason? In other words—forgive me, I'm being brutally frank, but—are you pregnant?'

Her face flamed. 'No! Of course I'm not!'

He looked totally unmoved. 'Then that gets the record straight. You're a very pretty girl, you know, with those brown eyes soft as moth's wings and that very volatile mouth—which I'd rather like to see when it's unpainted, by the way. I haven't seen you full length yet, but you look a slight and graceful five foot four. You must surely have had more than one love affair, more than one proposal—yet you've opted to marry someone you've never met. There's a great big "Please explain" buzzing round in my mind.' He tilted back his head and looked at her quizzically through half closed eyes that unnerved her quite as much as what he was saying, and she looked back at him blankly, unable to marshal her thoughts. The waitress brought the steaks and salads, which gave her a chance to recover her equilibrium, but as he attacked his food he pressed her, 'Well, let's hear your side of it.'

She bit her lip. 'Marriage isn't—as popular an end to a love affair as it used to be. Hasn't the news reached here yet? Maybe I've been unlucky, but the men who've dated me just haven't been interested in—legal tie-ups.'

He raised his eyebrows. 'So you pounced on my ad because you were fed up? Or because you can't do without sex and you want it to be legal?'

'No, of course not!' she exclaimed, angry that it was so easy for him to make her blush. 'I—I *was* fed up, but I didn't pounce on your ad. My flatmate pointed it out because she thought it might interest me.'

His eyes made another rapid tour of discovery. 'It's

still incredible, you know—a girl like you going in for mail order marriage.'

'Don't look at me as if I were a freak,' she said crossly. 'You were the one who put the ad in the paper in the first place—*you're* interested in mail order marriage and—and you're not exactly Dracula,' she enlarged, reflecting that it was a very decided understatement. She looked at him questioningly, because surely it was time he explained himself—they weren't going to talk about her all night.

'Okay, so I'm not,' he said, and spent the next few minutes on his dinner. Finally he raised his eyes. 'Anyhow, what was the catalyst to all this? Some particular man who let you down?'

'More or less.' She too had tried to get on with her dinner, but delicious though it was, her appetite seemed to have vanished.

'Are you teaching him a lesson? Or consigning him to limbo?'

She smiled faintly. 'Consigning him to limbo.'

'But in this particular way?—and against everyone's advice, I'm sure ... No parents, you said——'

'No. I haven't had parents since I was six years old. My grandmother brought me and my sister up. She was partially blind, so we grew up to be fairly self-reliant. I haven't told my sister what I'm doing now. She's married and lives down the coast in Wollongong, and I don't see a great deal of her. But my flatmate, Barbara Bennett—the one who showed me the ad—she thinks it's a mad thing to do.'

'Will she want to come to the wedding?' he asked, and Edie almost choked on a mouthful of food. The wedding! The way he said that, as though it were all cut and dried—no loopholes at all——

'I—don't know,' she said faintly.

'Do *you* want to make a social event out of it? Bridesmaids, confetti, guests, a three-tiered cake——'

'I—I hadn't thought about it,' she said bewilderedly. 'I—I don't suppose so.'

'Then that'll suit me ... Have you finished playing with your steak? Do you want a dessert or just coffee?'

'Just coffee, please,' she said weakly.

All the questions had been on his side, she thought a few minutes later, as they drank their coffee. All the answers had been on hers. One thing he hadn't asked, though, was whether she had changed her mind—or even whether she had made it up. She glanced at him covertly and felt her heart lurch at the sight of those dark glinting lashes, that heavy fall of smoky brown hair over a broad forehead, that mouth, so masculine yet so—emotive. What on earth was a man like that doing, advertising for a wife? There must be a catch somewhere—there had to be!

'When—I mean, how soon would you want me to —it to——'

Her voice faded away, and he frowned over his coffee and moved his spoon abstractedly to the other side of his saucer.

'As soon as it can be arranged.' He raised his eyes to hers and looked at her fully and candidly. 'You're not over-eager, are you?'

'Well, we—we've only just met,' she stammered.

'But by design,' he reminded her with a faint and unnerving smile. 'What I mean is, you're not exactly a frustrated female whose one big idea is to hurry through the formalities and get to bed with a man—any man.'

She flushed and caught her lip between her teeth. 'Did you—expect me to be like that?'

'Actually not. But of course you could have been. One never knows what's in a girl's mind when she writes to a perfect stranger agreeing to become his wife. It's something quite outside my experience to date.'

'So is meeting a man who's advertised for a wife outside mine,' she retorted confusedly, and he smiled crookedly.

'Touché! At all events, that's something I must talk to you about—but I think we could continue our conversation in a little more privacy . . . Are you ready?' he added, pushing back his chair and getting to his feet.

Edie did so too and discovered that her legs were shaking. She went ahead of him through the dining room and into the deserted lobby, wondering nervously if he was at last going to get around to telling her something about himself, or if she was simply expected to marry him blindfold, as it were. Though of course she wouldn't do that—not in a fit, she promised herself.

He took her arm. 'The worst of a small town like this is that there's nowhere much to go for a bit of privacy. I don't want to invite you to my room—it would be all round the district in no time. As it is, there's going to be a lot of speculation as to whether I picked you up in the dining room just now or whether we were acquainted before. However, that's not worrying me particularly . . . Would you object if we drove out of town and sat and talked in my car?'

'No. Should I?'

He raised his eyebrows. 'Well, you ought to know the answer to that. Run and fetch something to put around your shoulders, anyhow. I'll wait here for you.'

Edie vanished in the direction of her room. How different everything was from any of her vague imaginings! The crazy thing was that she hadn't the least idea what she was going to do next. The thought of marrying him was infinitely disturbing, and in her room she paused for an instant to look at herself in the

glass before finding a silky black shawl. She discovered
her cheeks were glowing and her eyes were bright, and
she knew that deep inside her she was wildly excited
against all reason—as if she were at the beginning of a
journey that just *could* turn out to be absolutely fan-
tastic, if only she didn't miss the boat—or step into
the water by mistake.

She flicked her shawl across her shoulders feeling
the cool smoothness of its touch, aware of an inward
thrill as she imagined it the touch of his hands ...

CHAPTER TWO

His car was a Ford Fairlane, big and comfortable and
quiet, and in a few minutes they had left the lights of
the small town behind them and were driving along a
flat, dead-straight road, gravel-surfaced, and lit only
by the stars. He pulled up finally in the deeper dark
under a huge tree by the roadside, switched off the
ignition, and turned to Edie. For a brief instant she
imagined he was going to take her in his arms, but she
was wrong.

'I suppose you're wondering what this is all about,'
he said.

'Yes.' She clasped her hands nervously and tried to
see his face, to match it to a voice that by now was
familiar and decidedly attractive.

'Well, I'm going to be quite honest with you—I don't
want you to accuse me of trickery.'

He paused, and she felt an odd thrill of apprehension run along her veins. 'What—what do you mean?'

Instead of answering, he asked, 'Do you smoke?'

'Hardly ever, but——'

'But you'd like a cigarette now? I would too.' Seconds passed while he lit first her cigarette and then his own, and then he leaned back in the seat and said, 'First of all, you know I'm a cattleman.'

'Yes, of course. And—and I know your cattle station is called Dhoora Dhoora. What does that mean?' she added, mainly out of nervousness.

'Roughly speaking, it means walkabout—or maybe a day's walk ... But it's not exactly *my* station, and that's more or less the crux of the matter. It's where you come in, in fact.'

'I don't know what you mean,' she said as he paused.

'I know you don't. But I'm about to tell you. I've lived on Dhoora Dhoora all my life. My father managed the outstation, and after he died, which was when I was sixteen, I moved over to the headquarters to live with my uncle, who was the boss and the owner. I started working on the place full time as soon as I left school, and I've run it for the past nine years or so— since my uncle's death.' He drew on his cigarette a couple of times, and Edie had the feeling he was working out what to say next, but so far she had no idea how she came into the picture.

'Philip, my uncle,' he resumed presently, 'was the eldest of the three Sutton sons, but he never married. That left me and my cousin Greg as the two possible heirs if the place was to be kept in the family—and it was something of an obsession with the old man that it should be—and that it shouldn't be divided up. Well, I had an advantage over Greg, although our fathers were twins, because I was the older by five years and more importantly, later on, because I was engaged to a girl of whom my uncle vastly approved.'

Edie felt a strange shock to know that he had been engaged, yet it would be impossible to imagine there had been no girls in his life, and she asked awkwardly, 'You—didn't marry her?'

'She died of meningitis a month before we were to have been married.'

'Oh, I'm sorry——'

He ignored her expression of sympathy and continued matter-of-factly, 'My uncle made a will in my favour after the engagement was announced, and shortly after, he died unexpectedly of a heart attack. In fairness to Greg—who, I forgot to tell you, lived and worked on the property too—he'd added a clause to his will that, if I were by some chance still unmarried by the time I was thirty-five, then Dhoora Dhoora was to go to Greg, provided *he* was married. You may find all this boring, but do you follow?'

'Yes.'

'Well then—when I tell you I'll be thirty-five on the eighteenth of next month, you'll understand why it is I need a wife in a hurry.'

Edie's lips parted in a silent gasp. In a curious and illogical way, she felt she'd been deceived. Because—because she'd pictured a lonely cattleman longing for a wife—though certainly that image had been shaken somewhat since she'd met him. She drew a deep slow breath and said evenly, 'Yes, I guess I do understand. I suppose your cousin's married already?'

'So far as I know, he's not. But you can count on it he'll be married before D-day.'

'He'll advertise too?' she asked with a humour that was forced.

'He won't need to,' Drew said abruptly. 'But before

you say the logical thing—that he has as much moral right to Dhoora Dhoora as I have—I'll make this point: He's taken absolutely no active interest in the property since my uncle died, even though we benefit from it equally. Next month the sharing period is ended—the station goes to one or the other of us, and this I know— that Greg will sell Dhoora Dhoora if he gets hold of it. My aunt will see to that.'

'I—see,' Edie said slowly. She saw why he didn't want his cousin to inherit, but she still didn't at all see why Drew had had to advertise for a wife. She felt certain there must be dozens of girls who would say yes to Drew Sutton if he asked them to marry him! As it was, Edie Asher, a perfect stranger, had been called in to save the day. And suppose she said no, that she didn't want to be in it?

He said into the darkness, 'What are you thinking? You surely can't be surprised to know that I have rational grounds for wanting a wife in a hurry?'

'I suppose not,' she agreed reluctantly. 'But—but you don't want a wife at all, really, do you? You just want to fulfil a condition, so you can inherit a cattle station.'

He laughed briefly. 'I want a wife—a family. I want to be able to hand Dhoora Dhoora on to my son. Oh yes, eventually I want a wife, Alfreda, make no mistake.'

In the darkness she saw him turn his head in her direction and she felt her breathing quicken as at the same moment she became burningly aware that his thigh was touching hers. She wanted to move, but she didn't do so. She didn't want him to know she was conscious of that point of physical contact.

'But of course,' she heard him say, 'I don't expect to get myself a wife *this* way. When I advertised my idea was to make a marriage that was simply a formality —a legal contract for the sake of expedience, an alliance that could be annulled once my affairs were settled. And by the way, I shall pay you a generous sum of money for services rendered,' he finished coolly.

Edie moved her position abruptly so as to break that unnerving contact with him that threatened to disturb her concentration.

'Don't you think it's a little unfair to—to trick someone into coming all this way for one thing and then explain that you want something quite—different?'

'Unfair?' he repeated, sounding surprised. 'No, I wouldn't call it that. A girl who answers an ad like mine is taking a big gamble anyway and should be very glad to escape with her virtue intact and a four-figure sum in her bank account. No, I don't think I'm being unfair at all. And from my own point of view, it's a sure and certain way of getting what I want.'

'But—what about me?' she asked, feeling a pulse begin to hammer at her temple.

'You? Haven't we more or less established that you're not a frustrated female? You won't end up on the shelf simply because *this* particular marriage isn't going to be a real one at any rate—I'll stake my life on it.'

'What if I tell you I've changed my mind—I don't want to go on with it?' she said huskily, and felt him move impatiently beside her.

'Now that I would take very badly,' he said, his voice harsh. 'Though short of literally twisting your arm or beating you up—and luckily for you I'm not the type to do that—I'm aware I can't force you to honour what I regard as a promise.'

'A promise?' she exclaimed. 'I didn't promise you anything!'

His broad shoulders lifted in a shrug. 'No? In my book you did. You came, didn't you? You knew you'd written the winning letter—you accepted the plane tickets, the cheque.'

'I haven't touched your cheque,' she broke in. 'It's in my pocketbook—I'll return it to you as soon as we go back to the hotel.'

'As you please.' There was a brief silence and then he said in a coldly level voice, 'Well, what's all the shilly-shallying about? *Are* you trying to tell me you're not going through with it? You were just amusing yourself, is that it?'

'No, I—I wasn't amusing myself. It wasn't anything like that.'

'No? You mean you really wanted to marry a stranger? Well then, suppose I were to say we'll make it a real marriage after all—you'd like that a whole lot better, would you? The idea of someone you know nothing about making love to you appeals to you, does it? Not necessarily me—just any cattleman of any age who wants a young and nubile woman in his bed.'

Edie swallowed hard. He sounded so hard, so cynical. Thoughts of arranged marriages flew wildly about inside her head. She had been so eager to persuade herself they worked, that she wasn't really doing anything so extraordinary or impossible. But she was, of course, and when she thought what kind of a man he could have been—and what he could have asked of her—she shuddered to her very soul. She wished now that she had kept quiet, too, and not babbled on about unfairness.

'Well, does it?' he insisted, and the next moment he had caught hold of her shoulders and twisted her round in the seat till she was facing him and so close she could feel the warmth of his breath on her forehead. He held her so hard she was helpless and she stayed rigid with shock, waiting for what he might do next.

'Now listen to me, Edie,' he grated. 'I picked your letter out from the various answers I got for several reasons. You appeared to be free of possibly disapproving relatives, and as well, you weren't being enticed away from some job you couldn't go back to later. As a nurse, I calculated, you must have some intelligence, and you'd understand my dilemma and even sympathise with it. What I didn't count on—not for a split second—was that you'd be a beautiful girl with the kind of sensitive and subtle feminity that could well be any man's undoing. Believe me, it would be no punishment to me to make love to you, if that's what you want, and I think I can promise you a fair amount of satisfaction. So——'

Her heart thudding, she put her hands on his chest and tried desperately to push him away from her.

'I don't—I don't want you to make love to me——'

'Then what the hell do you want? And don't for God's sake resort to tears. I'm as serious about this business as I ever was about anything in the whole of my life. So you tell me exactly what you want and we'll make some sort of an arrangement that gives us both what we want. Because believe me, I'm going to have what *I* want, some way or other.'

Tears had flown to her eyes, but she blinked them back angrily. She felt so shaken she didn't know how to answer him. It would be so easy to say weakly, 'I want to go home,' and to burst into tears, but he made it plain he wouldn't tolerate that. No way could he get what he wanted if she went home, and the thing was, he had been perfectly right in what he had said. The very fact that she had come here was evidence of her willingness to marry him. But it would be embarrassing now to insist that *she* wanted it to be a real marriage. Besides, she didn't—of course she didn't! Meanwhile, his fingers were hurting her shoulders badly, and she searched her mind desperately to find words to answer his demand.

At last she said shakily, 'I certainly don't want to be married to you—really married! You—you look nice enough, but I think you're too much of a—a brute for my tastes. I don't even know how much you really deserve this station you're using such tricks to get ... But I don't want to be beaten up or to have my arm twisted, so I'll do what you insist I've promised to do, I suppose. I'll marry you the way you said, and the sooner we break it up and part, the happier I'll be.'

She heard his brief mirthless laugh as he shook her slightly and let her go.

'It's a shame I have to hold you to your promise, *Miss Asher*, and I won't modify the compliment I paid you a moment ago, though I'm very much tempted to do so. You're very fortunate, if you'd only realise it. You should be thanking your lucky stars you haven't fallen into the clutches of a lecher ... In a minute or two I'll take you back into town, but first of all I'll let you know my arrangements. I've already applied for a special licence so we can be married at Mount Isa in a few days' time. I'll want some details from you—I'll let you have the relevant papers and you can fill them in when we go back to the hotel. Between now and our —wedding day you'll have a choice of staying in Narrunga or coming back with me to Dhoora Dhoora, but under the circumstances, I think you'd better opt for the latter.'

Because, of course, she might run out on him if he left her on her own. And so she might.

'All right,' she said stiffly. 'Whatever you say, Mr Sutton.'

'I had thought you might like to come to Dhoora Dhoora,' he said, and his voice was subdued and meditative so that something in her responded and went out to him in an odd way. She didn't know what had gone wrong and she wished it hadn't, and she wished too he hadn't talked to her so brutally when it could all have been so civilised. 'I thought you might like a taste of outback life,' he added. 'I'd imagined we could get to know something about each other and make an agreeable and pleasant thing of our brief partnership. However'—he moved to switch on the motor and the headlights, 'don't upset yourself. I shan't bother you more than I can help.'

'Thank you,' she said aloofly, wishing futilely that they could somehow go back to the point in their exchange where it had all gone out of control—the point, perhaps, where she had suggested she might change her mind and he had become so ruthless and determined. Why had she said that? she wondered, as he turned the car and they headed back to town. Was it sheer feminine perversity because he had taken it for granted that everything was settled?—because he hadn't done her the courtesy of asking her if she still wanted to go ahead?

Neither of them said anything further, and Edie was relieved when at last the lights of Narrunga appeared. For a girl who believed in marriage—in legal tie-ups —she reflected bitterly, she was giving herself a very strange deal indeed.

Edie woke the next morning feeling dull and subdued. She had dealt with the papers Drew Sutton had handed her last night when they came back to the hotel, and then they had parted for the night. Her sleep had been restless, her dreams confused, and she had wakened several times during the night to the feeling that her life had gone sour. She tried to persuade herself that she shouldn't be upset, that she should be glad she wasn't after all expected to make a real marriage with a man she didn't know.

After she had showered and dressed, she made up her mind to make a fresh start, to cheer up, and to apologise to Drew Sutton for the unpleasantness of last night, and even to accept the full blame for it. He wasn't asking a great deal of her, after all, and he had been honest about his requirements, and it was a situation she could accept if she looked at it sensibly.

He wasn't about when she went along to the dining room, and she concluded he had gone to finish making the arrangements for their wedding. What a farce, she thought nervily, as she ate her breakfast. But she had no one to blame but herself. She should never have been so silly—or so naïve—as to answer an advertisement like that.

Later, in her room, she packed the few things she had taken from her suitcase, then sat down at the dressing table to write a brief letter to Barb, telling her that she wasn't being rushed to the altar, that they had both been quite wrong about Drew Sutton, that everything was fine and she was going to spend a few days at Dhoora Dhoora and would be in touch later. She supposed she would have to tell Barb about the marriage she was going to contract, but she wouldn't tell her until it was an accomplished fact, or she might come racing up to stop it. As for the pay-off she had been promised—four figures—she didn't want Drew Sutton's money. Even the cheque he had sent her was all ready inside her handbag to be given back the moment she saw him again.

She was coming back from the post office when a car pulled up beside her, and of course it was Drew. She felt the colour rush to her face and her legs turn to water, and though she told herself it was because of the chilliness between them last night, she knew in her heart it also had a lot to do with the fact that he was such an ultra-good-looking and virile man, and that those extraordinary eyes of his had such a disturbing effect on her.

'Been posting letters?' he asked, leaning across to open the car door for her.

'Just one,' she said awkwardly. 'To Barbara—my flatmate.' Then, anticipating his question, she added, 'I didn't tell her the whole story. Just that I was here and —safe and sound.'

He smiled wryly but made no comment and as the car moved on down the street she turned her head to look at him. 'I'm sorry about last night,' she said with forced brightness. 'About making such a fuss, I mean. Of course I'll—help you out.'

He looked straight ahead of him. 'Forget it. I guess you just didn't know if you were on your head or your heels,' he said casually.

So he was letting her take all the blame, she thought with slight resentment.

'I've got everything lined up for Friday,' he added after a moment. 'It will be a register office wedding. You know that, don't you? I can't very well expect you to promise to love, honour and obey me until death us do part under the circumstances, can I?'

'No,' she agreed, and looked at him sideways. 'It was very trusting of you to leave me on my own this morning.'

She saw his eyebrows rise. 'Not all that trusting. I thought you were sufficiently chastened.'

'Did you?' she said, feeling her anger flare. 'I've been counting my blessings, as a matter of fact. I'm having a lucky escape in a way. I wouldn't *choose* to marry a man like you in a million years.'

'It would certainly be a very long chance we should be compatible under the circumstances, wouldn't it?' he said maddeningly. 'Personally I wouldn't expect to find a soulmate by such a hit-or-miss method.'

'You haven't,' she said briefly.

He turned his head and sent her a crooked smile. 'No doubt we'll both make one or two discoveries during the next few weeks ...'

They left for Dhoora Dhoora that afternoon—a drive of a hundred and ninety-five kilometres over a gravel road that didn't make for fast travelling. Drew had commented as he loaded her luggage into the car, 'You travel light, don't you?'

'I'm glad I do,' she retorted. 'I'd have looked a fool if I'd brought everything with me, wouldn't I?—just for a few weeks.'

They arrived at Dhoora Dhoora before sunset. A wide gate gave on to the gravel road, and above the gate, in metal letters, was the name Dhoora Dhoora. Edie felt a strange little thrill go through her as they drove through. Walkabout, Drew had said it meant. Somehow she liked that. Not that it mattered to her in the least, she amended her thoughts hastily.

There was a cylindrical mail box, a cattle grid, a narrow red road that ran beside a post and wire fence and passed, she soon discovered, through several gates that had to be opened and then shut. At either side, vast paddocks stretched out to eternity—gently heaving paddocks, covered with Mitchell grass. Going on for ever and ever, Edie thought—rolling over the horizon, on and on, dotted with cattle and with a feathery sort of scrub that looked light enough to blow away if the slightest wind arose—an illusion, of course, because it was very tough and very solid and had to be, to survive out here. On the edge of the world, trees floated—trunkless, ephemeral, wavering like balloons on strings.

'It's a big property, isn't it?' she commented as she climbed back into the car after closing the third gate.

'Not so big as it once was,' said Drew. 'Dhoora Dhoora was twice the size it is now in my great-grandfather's time, but his two sons weren't equally interested, and one half of the place was sold. That's why my grandfather left it solely to his eldest son—my uncle—and incidentally, why he wanted to leave it solely to either me or my cousin Greg.'

'I see,' she said uncomfortably, remembering how she had at least by implication cast doubt on his reasons for wanting to gain possession.

'I told you I was engaged to Deborah Webster,' he remarked presently. 'The reason my uncle was so delighted about that was because it was the Webster family who'd bought the other half of Dhoora Dhoora, and since Debbie was the only child, my uncle saw the property being restored to its previous size. But it was not to be,' he finished sombrely.

'I suppose——' she began, and then stopped.

'You suppose what?'

'Nothing,' she murmured, and Drew didn't pursue it. She'd been going to suggest that the reason he hadn't married was because he had never got over Deborah's death, but it wasn't her business and it could be that he still hadn't got over it.

After the fourth gate, a cluster of silvery roofs appeared across a yellow plain, their colour merging into the silver of cloud in a vast sky as yet not flooded by the red of sunset. Edie wondered how it would feel if this was—coming home. He must be proud of Dhoora Dhoora, she thought, and she could fully understand his not wanting to lose it. Though the country looked harsh and the trees were wild and scrubby-looking, it had always been home to him. She felt the first real twinge of sympathy with Drew Sutton. He would be really cut up if his cousin inherited and sold the place.

'What would you do if your cousin—if Dhoora Dhoora went to your cousin and he put it up for sale?' she asked musingly. 'Would you—buy it?'

'My dear girl, I couldn't afford it,' he said with asperity. 'No, some pastoral company would buy it up —the same impersonal company, perhaps, that now owns Quabin Downs, since the Websters have gone. They'd put a manager in and the boss would come out for a week or so every year to look through the books with an accountant.'

She digested that, then asked, 'What *would* you do, then? Wouldn't you stand a good chance of being appointed manager?'

He turned his brilliant grey eyes on her, narrowed and blackly lashed, and one eyebrow peaked sardonically. 'D'you think that would make me happy, Alfreda?'

'I—I guess it wouldn't.'

'You're damned right.'

'Then what *would*——'

'Look,' he interrupted savagely, 'it might amuse you to play this guessing game, but I'm not interested in speculation. I'll get myself a wife before the eighteenth of next month no matter how ruthless I have to be. And if you're still considering slipping the noose from around your neck, then you'd better tell me right away and I'll turn this vehicle round and take you back to

Narrunga.' His foot went down violently on the brake as he spoke and the car pulled up with a neck-breaking jerk that left Edie shaken. Drew swung round in the seat to confront her. 'Well? Make up your mind. And if you're going to think up any more hypothetical questions such as what I'll do if you walk out on me, then get this quite straight in your mind—you aren't the only fish in the sea and you don't hold my future in the palm of your hand. No woman on this earth does that. I hazarded a guess that you'd be a decent sort of a girl to deal with, but if you opt out now, I'll take a chance on another of the several ladies who were apparently eager and willing to marry a cattleman. But this time I'll have learned my lesson and I won't play it so straight down the middle. In fact, I'll save the honesty until after the wedding's over.' He paused and looked at her hard. 'Well? Do you want me to take you back to Narrunga?'

Edie stared at him, completely taken aback. She hadn't thought of opting out—not now—but when he spoke to her like that, she longed to do so. He wasn't the slightest bit diplomatic or tactful, and as far as she could see, he didn't even like her.

'Well?' he snapped out impatiently. 'Can't you make up your mind one way or the other? What's bugging you now, anyway? Are you afraid I have plans to take advtantage of you—attack your virtue?'

She turned away from him abruptly. The colour had left her face and she clasped her trembling hands in her lap and said with an attempt to keep her voice even, 'Mr Sutton, if I walked out on you now, it would —it would just serve you right. You're—you're positively unpleasant! I've already told you I'd carry out my obligations. I didn't breathe one single word just now about not going through with this pretence of a marriage. *You're* the one who put your foot on the brake. I was—I was simply asking a few questions out of interest. But if you don't trust me or can't stand the sight of me, then do as you please. I don't care. Take me back to Narrunga—catch yourself another fish——' Her voice had begun to shake and she stopped speaking and bit hard on her lip.

After a second she heard him sigh. Then he reached out and took hold of her arm and pulled her round to face him.

'Okay, I'll say it—I'm sorry. I'm on edge over this whole business, I guess, and you're just not the slightly wacky rather nice little nurse I'd imagined I was getting hold of, a sensible girl who'd be satisfied with a nest egg. There's something about you that unsettles me. As from now, I'll watch it.'

'I—I wish you would,' she said, hating the fact that her lower lip was quivering, and hating even more the fact that he had obviously noticed it. 'Who'll be at the homestead when we get there?' she asked, determinedly changing the subject.

One corner of his mouth lifted in a sudden smile. 'Don't worry, you won't have to put on a show tonight. My housekeeper doesn't live in. She's the boreman's wife and they have their own bungalow. She keeps my house tidy with the help of a couple of aboriginal girls, and she cooks my dinner, but otherwise she leaves me alone.'

Edie swallowed. 'You mean—there'll just be you and—me?'

'Yes. But don't let that upset you. It will be the same way after we're married—I'll want you to live at Dhoora Dhoora, of course.' He let go of her arm as if suddenly aware he was holding it. 'We'd better get moving again,' he said. 'You're looking tired.'

She was tired. Tired enough to want to have a good

cry, but of course that wouldn't be allowed. Not till tonight when she'd gone to bed and could cry privately into her pillow—alone in the house with *him* ...

A few minutes later the homestead came into sight. Grouped around it were various smaller buildings which Drew pointed out as the store, the workshop, the shed for the plant. As well there were several bungalows—for the boreman, the stockmen, the cook and so on. It was almost a little village and the hub of it all, though set apart in its sheltering trees, was the big ranch-like homestead, with deep, creeper-shaded verandahs, a rose garden and a tennis court.

As they left the car, Edie had a feeling of nervousness. She wondered how she would have felt if the marriage ahead of her was to have been a real one instead of a mere formality designed to serve a very practical purpose. For sure she'd have felt even more trepidation than she did now. Imagine living with this dynamic, maddening man as his wife—sharing his bed——

The housekeeper, Mrs Wilson, came into the hall and Drew introduced her to Edie so casually that Edie had the distinct impression she had been told about her. Though exactly what she had been told it was impossible to guess.

'Carry on with dinner,' Drew said presently, and added humorously, 'It smells good enough to eat!'

Mrs Wilson smiled and vanished in the direction of the kitchen, and Edie, her cheeks slightly flushed, asked him, 'What have you told her about me?'

'What do you think?' He raised his straight thick eyebrows and looked at her quizzically. 'That you're my fiancée, of course. But don't worry, she doesn't know how I got hold of you. She has no part in my personal life.'

'I thought—in the outback—everyone was on equal terms,' Edie said tentatively as she followed him along the hallway.

'You mean you imagined she'd be calling me by my christian name and warning me that no good would come of getting a missus this way? Well, perhaps fortunately, Mrs Wilson is more or less a newcomer here. However, I haven't confided in anyone what I've been doing, if it's of any comfort to you. So don't worry that the housekeeper will be bringing a pile of socks to darn while you and I are having coffee in the sitting room after dinner. As soon as she's fixed whatever it is she's cooking in the kitchen, she'll vamoose and get Frank's tucker on the go ... This is your room,' he concluded, pushing open a door and standing aside.

Edie's nerves tingled. Very soon she and Drew Sutton would be quite alone, and the thought was a distinctly disquieting one. What would they talk about over dinner—afterwards? The less they talked, the better, she thought. They seemed to have acquired very quickly a habit of misunderstanding each other. Or at least, he misunderstood her. She had already misunderstood him, of course, thanks to his apparently unambiguous advertisement that had, after all, meant something entirely different from what it had stated. She was of two minds as to whether she should be thankful about that or not ...

He said into her thoughts, 'Unpack all your things if you want to—you've plenty of time. I'll give you a call when dinner's ready.'

'Thank you,' she said, and added desperately, 'Won't there be anyone else with us? I mean, the—the jackeroos, the——'

'Nobody,' he said emphatically. 'Definitely not. They're out at the muster camp in any case. But even when they're here, this is my private home. It's a big cattle station, Alfreda, big enough still to have an out-station, as I think I told you earlier—forty or fifty kilometres from here ... You'll find a bathroom at the end of the hall. It's been renovated lately—that and the kitchen, so it's one up on the little bathroom at the end of the verandah. I'll be taking my shower there.'

'Great,' she thought frantically. 'At least we shan't be sharing a bathroom.'

With a smile he left her, and she drew a deep breath and for the first time really looked about her. It was a big room, a handsome room. The carpet, grey with a pattern of roses, was slightly faded but obviously of first-rate quality. The curtains were faded too, and so was the bedspread on a double bed that had an elegantly carved bedhead and two matching bedside tables. A door opened on to the verandah and two wide low-silled windows looked across to the rose garden.

Edie started her unpacking, uncertain as to how much she should take out of her suitcases. But after all, she was going to marry him, wasn't she? She was going to live here for the next few weeks. Abruptly she switched off her thoughts. It was madness to think about the situation too much. Mindlessly, she began to hang her dresses in the big carved wardrobe that looked as if it weighed about a ton, and to put her neatly folded underthings away in the chest of drawers. She tried not to look at the double bed, though certainly she would be sleeping there alone, even after they were married. Or so Drew said.

Presently she went along to the bathroom to wash and after she came back to her room she slipped outside on an impulse to cut a couple of dark red roses with her nail scissors. When she was dressed, she pinned one of them to the shoulder of the cream blouse

she was wearing with a long flowered skirt. She was
fixing the second rose in her hair when Drew tapped on
the door and came in, and Edie flushed deeply as his
reflection joined hers in the mirror. Her arms were
raised as she clipped the rose in position with a
tortoiseshell clasp that had belonged to her grandmother, and the stuff of her blouse, pulled tight, revealed the points of her breasts. Through the mirror,
Drew was looking at her body in a curiously pro-
prietorial way, and she fastened the clip clumsily and
swung away from the glass.

'I like the scent you use,' he said as she straightened
the belt that encircled her narrow waist. 'It matches
your personality.'

She looked at him warily through her lashes. 'It's
not scent. It's these roses—from your garden. I—I
picked two. Is that all right?'

'Of course. Go for your life—cut all you want ... I
came to tell you dinner's ready, and in case you're feeling shy of Mrs Wilson, she's gone.'

In other words they were alone. And he had felt
himself quite at liberty to come into her room. She
could feel herself bristling as she went ahead of him
through the doorway and she tossed over her shoulder,
'By the way, I'd rather you didn't come into my bedroom like that.'

'Not before we're married?' he said mockingly from
behind her.

'Nor afterwards,' she said tightly. His hand was
under her elbow as he directed her into the dining room
where the table was laid for two. It was dark now,
and candles burned in silver candlesticks. It looked
romantic and Edie supposed that Mrs Wilson had
meant it that way. But there was certainly no romance
between Edie Asher and Drew Sutton.

As she slid into the chair he pulled out for her she looked up at him and said coolly, 'I'm doing you a favour, you know. I do expect to be able to dictate some of the terms.'

'Dictate?' he repeated. 'That's a word I don't like.' He sat down opposite her and his grey eyes looked at her unreadably across the candlelight. 'I don't want to have everything my way, but all the same don't assume I'm ready to fall over myself to please or placate you, for fear you might walk out on me. I'm just not the grovelling type.'

'I've noticed that,' she retorted. 'But neither am I. I'll honour my promise, but I expect you to honour yours as well.'

'I'll do my best,' he said with an odd half smile. 'But you might need to remind me of it now and again ... Help yourself to the casserole. It's beef olives, something Mrs Wilson appears to do rather well, and rather often.' He lifted the lid of the blue patterned dish as he spoke and a tempting smell drifted across the table. Edie helped herself, and from another covered dish took a serving of vegetables. The table was a long one, and their places were laid intimately close at one end. Long curtains had been drawn across the windows so that the two of them were closed in, in a world that was very intimate and very private. Edie worried inwardly over what Drew had said about reminding him of his promise, but instead of following it up she asked with a sigh as she started her dinner, 'What does the boreman do, Drew?'

'He looks after the bores,' he said with a comical lift of his brows. 'We depend largely on bore water for our stock on Dhoora Dhoora. It's pumped up from underground into storage tanks, then channelled out for the cattle. The boreman's job is to check that the pumps are operating and that there's always water when the cattle come to drink. Frank Wilson is the station mechanic as well—he looks after all the vehicles and the electricity generator. He's only been employed here a few weeks, but I'm very satisfied with him.'

'Who did your housekeeping before Mrs Wilson came?' Edie asked curiously.

'The last mechanic's wife. They left because she wasn't too happy here. Mrs Wilson's used to the outback and she looks like being a real winner, so I'm in luck. It's not always easy to get good staff—or to keep it. In fact, a wife—of the right kind—can be a definite asset,' he concluded, his eyes surveying her enigmatically across the table.

'It's a wonder you haven't found yourself one long ago,' she said involuntarily, and his look darkened.

'I'll be remedying that very shortly, shan't I?'

'Not at all!' she exclaimed. 'I shan't be your wife—and you said it would be for only a few weeks——'

'That was the original idea,' he agreed, and added irritatingly, 'Though it appeared to take you a while to reconcile yourself to it.'

'Don't worry, I'm quite reconciled since—since making your acquaintance,' she said swiftly, then determinedly returned her attention to her meal.

'It's very good steak, isn't it?' she commented, after a long silence.

'Very good,' he agreed dryly.

She didn't stay up for long after dinner but excused herself and went to her room—though once there she felt more nervous than in his presence. Why, she couldn't really imagine. If he merely wanted to marry her in order to gain possession of Dhoora Dhoora, then she should be perfectly safe. But he looked so virile, she was so intensely aware of the fact that he was a male, she couldn't escape from the fact that she was alone in the house with him. Terribly alone.

Once during the night she woke with a start to the uneasy feeling that he was there in the room, but when she sat up and reached for the switch on the bedside lamp, the room was empty.

CHAPTER THREE

IT was with a mixture of relief and resentment that Edie discovered she was to see very little of Drew during the two days they were to spend at Dhoora Dhoora before the wedding. He spent both of those days out at the muster camp, and since he left the homestead before she woke in the morning, and didn't come home till close on sundown, for Edie the day was lonely and long.

The first morning, she had finished her breakfast of tea and toast before Mrs Wilson came to wash the breakfast and dinner dishes, which Drew had insisted last night she should leave. With her came the two aboriginal girls, shy and inclined to giggle, and taking their time over the sweeping and polishing and dusting Mrs Wilson directed them to do. Edie, sitting on the verandah, more or less on the edge of her chair, and feeling she shouldn't be there at all, thought that if she had really been Drew's fiancée she'd have been eager to learn how to manage the household and the girls. As it was, she kept well away from the activities, and

Mrs Wilson didn't bother her, merely coming through to tell her, before she left, that there was cold meat and salad in the refrigerator for her lunch.

After that, the house was empty again, and presently Edie put on her wide-brimmed hat and went through the garden, past the tennis court and away from the sheltering trees—the bauhinias, the pink and white oleanders, the great mango trees laden with ripening fruit—to see what she could see. It was a big wide world of silence and hot sunshine, the horizons drifting away to nowhere, shimmering in the heat. She saw a man in a paddock where there were a number of horses, but she didn't go and speak to him, and beyond that she saw no one but a few aboriginal children playing in the sand in the shade of the trees. She wondered if any of the stockmen's wives were about, but under the circumstances didn't want to seek them out, and though she heard parrots chattering and the million voices of a flock of green budgerigars crowding across the sky, she heard little else.

She wondered when Drew would be home, but she hadn't liked to ask Mrs Wilson and couldn't bring herself to do so when she came to the house in the afternoon to prepare dinner. It would seem very odd having to ask questions about your own fiancée.

He came at sundown, and by then she was once more ensconced on the verandah, edgy and feeling decidedly keyed up. Drew came up the steps, paused as he reached the verandah, lit a cigarette, and looked at her levelly across the flame of his lighter.

'Did you have a quiet day?' he asked, and those brilliant grey eyes of his examined her openly.

'Very quiet,' she agreed, and somehow managed a smile.

He came to lean against the rails closer to her.

'Did you miss me?'

Her nerves jumped and colour flared in her cheeks. 'What do you think?' she retorted—then suddenly wondered if he were talking this way for Mrs Wilson's benefit, in case she was within earshot. A little disconcerted, she glanced towards the sitting room doors, which were open wide. No one was there, she was sure, but she asked Drew pleasantly, 'How did you spend the day?'

'I went out to the muster camp. Ordinarily, I'd have stayed there with the men tonight, but with you here I can hardly do that.'

'No,' she said uneasily. 'What are they—the men—doing at the muster camp?'

'Rounding up the cattle. Marking the calves with the Dhoora Dhoora brand and the year so we can keep tabs on their age. Drafting out the beasts that aren't good breeders—they'll be sold. Mustering goes on most of the year for various reasons—both from here and from the outstation at the western end of the run. I like to be in it—but of course I must take time off to get married,' he finished sardonically.

Edie looked away from him. 'Do they—do they know you're getting married?'

'Sure they know—if by "they" you mean the stockmen. But don't worry, they don't expect to be asked to the wedding ... Anyhow, what did you do with yourself all day?'

'Nothing,' she said, curling her fingers into her palms and looking at her nails—which she had lacquered about an hour ago for want of anything better to do. 'What did you expect me to do?'

'I thought you might have been inquisitive enough to poke around and see what you could find out. In fact, I half expected to hear you'd been out riding. Harry—

the yard man—would have saddled up a horse for you if you'd asked him.'

'I don't ride,' she said, reflecting that the man she had seen in the horse paddock must have been Harry.

His eyebrows rose. 'No? Oh well, I should have guessed. Tennis and swimming are your sports, aren't they? I'm afraid it's too late for a game of tennis this evening. In fact, if you'll excuse me, I'd better get under the shower or dinner will be on the table and I shan't be ready.'

'Go ahead,' said Edie. He crushed out his cigarette in an ashtray on a table near her chair, and she watched him stride away and tried to analyse her feelings. But they were completely unanalysable. She knew she was finding the situation both unreal and difficult to accept and she had the impression that Drew wished she were different in some way, but she didn't know how. Perhaps he'd have preferred it if she'd been more sanguine, more amused, instead of being so touchy, as she undoubtedly was.

'I'll be glad when it's all over,' she told herself, and getting up determinedly, went into the garden.

She was still there when dinner was ready and Drew came to find her.

'No roses tonight?' he asked dryly, and she shook her head. The roses smelled swooningly sweet, but she hadn't bothered going inside for scissors and was disconcerted now when he pulled a red rose himself—a half opened bud—and handed it to her with a kind of mocking gallantry.

'It's definitely your flower, Edie. Have you a brooch or a pin?'

'I'm afraid I haven't.' She turned away swiftly from the look in his eyes as they went to her breast, and began to move towards the house. She didn't wear the rose, but in the dining room laid it on the table—and left it there.

Dinner passed uneventfully, and afterwards Drew disappeared to the office—'To do some paper work,' he said. Edie sat alone in the sitting room, with the radio playing and a writing pad on her lap and a feeling of resentment in her mind.

She didn't see him again that night. After an hour or so on her own, she went to bed. He wasn't going to find her waiting meekly for him when his work was finished —not after being ignored like that. She shut her door, got into her pyjamas, climbed into bed, switched off the light and lay there seething. Surely he owed it to her to be just a little bit attentive—presenting her with a rose was hardly enough. She was doing him a favour after all, and right now she couldn't think how she had fallen for it, how he had talked her into it. One thing was for sure, once it was all over, she wouldn't waste a moment getting away from here—and from him ...

The next evening when he came home she deliberately made a point of not being there to meet him. In fact, she was in her bedroom, dressed ready for dinner. She heard the sound of the jeep, and then she heard him come on to the verandah and call her name— 'Edie!' Commandingly, it seemed to her. Who did she think he was, for heaven's sake? She didn't answer, not even when he called again, this time from inside the house. Instead, she slipped through the verandah door and went into the rose garden. The sky was red and the garden was alive with dramatic colour, and she stood staring around her, wondering why her heart was beating so fast.

It beat even faster when he appeared—gilded by the sun, alarmingly male, intent on her.

'Are you playing hide and seek with me?' he demanded roughly. 'Didn't you hear me come in?'

'Yes, I—I heard you,' she said defiantly. 'But I didn't think you'd particularly want to see me.'

The expression in his grey eyes changed subtly to one she didn't understand. 'Didn't you? Well, as it happens, I've been looking forward to it on and off all day long. You're definitely a feast for sore eyes, you know. You can have no idea what the thought of coming home to someone like you can mean to a man who's out in the heat all day—riding with a lot of tough stockmen, jostling about in dust churned up by a mob of cattle. I've thought of the sheen of your hair and the scent of your skin—and the soft curves of your body—a million times since sun-up.'

Edie turned away, her cheeks scarlet. She felt deeply disturbed to hear him talk that way. It—it shook her. She wished now, whatever she'd wished before, that he'd keep the whole thing the way it was meant to be, strictly impersonal, strictly businesslike. She said disdainfully, though shakily, 'How can you talk such—such absolute rubbish? Do you think I *want* you to talk to me like that? I don't, you know. Especially just now,' she added, her brown eyes taking in the checked shirt clinging to his muscular torso, the dust stains on his narrow-legged cord pants, the dirt on his face. 'You surely can't think you're very attractive when you're covered in dust and sweat.'

She saw a flash of anger fire in his eyes and smoulder still as he answered. 'I might be a little more so when I've washed away the smell of my sweat and got into clean clothes, perhaps, Edie Asher. Is that it? Well, I'm a cattleman, not a city clerk, in case you've forgotten, and the way I feel right now I'm not inclined to wait—to store it all up.' He reached out unexpectedly and grabbed her wrist, pulling her to him with a rough

movement that almost knocked her off her feet. Her
heart leaped, her pulses pounded, and a feeling of wild
excitement coursed through her veins. Held this way,
with one arm doubled against his chest, she could feel
the heat and the dampness of his sweat as well as the
thump of his heartbeat. His fingers, rough with dust,
rasped against her smooth clean skin, and her nostrils
flared sensitively as she closed her eyes faintingly
against the expression on his face—the sensual twist of
his mouth.

She gasped out, 'I—I really don't think I find cattlemen attractive at all, Mr Sutton.'

'No? Then you've left your discovery a bit late,
haven't you? You knew what I was when you wrote to
me so prettily,' he said thickly. He had jerked her arm
behind her back and now he captured her other wrist,
and brought the full length of her body into suffocatingly close contact with his own. Her eyes flew open
and she took in the tiny lines on his face—beside his
mouth, radiating out from his eyes, each one drawn in
finely in red dust—dust that followed the curve of
his nostrils too, and blurred with its film the customary
glitter of his dark eyelashes. She tried to feel repelled,
but instead that mad excitement surged up in her again.
She had never been held so brutally by a man before,
never been so close to a male who looked so earthy and
acted so rough. Instinctively, her eyes sought his
mouth, then went to the day's growth of beard on his
jaw, dark and intensely masculine, and she caught her
breath as suddenly he held her harder against him and
his mouth came down on hers.

His hands were flat on her back, crushing her body
to his, and a physical response ran through her swift
and painful as an electric current. The touch of his lips

made her discover almost shockingly nerve centres she had never before been aware of.

It was seconds before she recovered her senses enough to pull away from him and to wipe her mouth hard with the knuckles of one hand.

'What—what did you do that for?'

'Do what? Kiss you?' He said it so flatly she recoiled inwardly. Kiss her! Was that what he called it? 'I wouldn't have thought that would be open to question, seeing we're being married tomorrow. It's unthinkable that a girl should go unkissed to her own wedding, now isn't it?'

'Don't be so—infuriating!' she exclaimed. 'Ours isn't going to be that kind of a marriage.'

'Well, you never know,' he said calmly. 'Anyhow, the temptation was quite irresistible.'

She could hear her own breathing. 'You'll just have to learn to resist it, I'm afraid, Mr Sutton. I don't find you—attractive.'

His mouth curved in a slow smile. 'Unpalatable words! Well, I'll get rid of the dust and sweat, shall I?'

'I couldn't care less whether you do or not!' she exclaimed, but she said it to his back, for he was already striding through the garden in the direction of the house. She watched him go with a confusion of emotions. Her nerves felt tangled and her legs were shaking. The thought that tomorrow she was to be married to him was utterly unbelievable. She couldn't think how she had been so weak as to get herself into such a situation—nor could she think why she didn't simply refuse to go on with the charade.

They were married the following day in Mount Isa, in a civil ceremony. Edie wore a cream lace blouse and a pale blue skirt, while Drew was in a lightweight beige suit with a finely striped shirt and a plain navy tie. He looked excruciatingly handsome and she knew that the witnesses who had been called in from the street thought them a good-looking couple.

But to Edie it was all like some mad thing she was dreaming, and she was convinced that when she went outside into the burning sunshine with Drew she would suddenly wake up and find herself back in the flat with Barb. But of course she didn't.

They had flown over from Narrunga in the afternoon, and since they had arrived in town barely a quarter of an hour before the time fixed for the marriage, she had scarcely had a moment to consider what happened next. But now with a ring on her finger and legs that persisted in feeling distinctly wobbly, she began to wonder nervily what plans the man beside her —her husband!—had made for their wedding night.

'We'll have a little celebration dinner at the hotel,' he told her at exactly that instant, glancing at his watch. 'A drink first. I guess you feel like a drink, Alfreda.'

Yes, at that moment Edie badly needed a drink, though she wasn't the sort of girl who resorted to alcohol. She asked nervously, 'When will we be flying back to Narrunga, Drew?'

'Tomorrow,' he said briefly. 'We're spending tonight at the hotel here. It will be a very short honeymoon,' he added dryly, 'but there's work waiting for me back home at Dhoora Dhoora.'

Edie swallowed hard. A night at the hotel with him! He had hired a car, and now he installed her gallantly in the front seat and climbed in beside her while she watched him edgily.

'We—we don't need a honeymoon at all,' she said. 'Why can't we go straight back to Dhoora Dhoora?'

'You'd have preferred that?' He sent her a glittering

sideways glance from his ice grey eyes.

Edie didn't know what to say. She was, frankly, too mixed up to know if she'd have preferred to go straight back 'home', or if it would have been any less nerve-racking.

'Don't worry,' Drew said almost soothingly when she didn't answer. 'I really haven't forgotten the terms of our union.'

Of course he hadn't! What on earth had she been imagining? That he was going to force himself on her —make love to her? She gave a sickly smile and said with difficulty as he drove along the wide street, 'I hope you've booked separate rooms.'

'I'm sorry, but I haven't. That would be going too far—we do have appearances to keep up,' he said abruptly.

She sank back in the seat biting her lip, and after a quick glance, he told her impatiently, 'Don't make too much of a thing of it, for heaven's sake. Why don't you try to see the rainbow at the end—the pot of gold? Picture yourself in twelve months or so marrying some handsome young guy from the city—won't you be pleased then you've got a nice little cache stowed away to buy yourself some of the good things you'd like in your home? Good God, you'll think of me with friendliness and gratitude then. Nothing terrible's going to happen to you after all, is it?'

No, he was right, nothing terrible was going to happen to her—though exactly what *was* going to happen she didn't care to think about. She couldn't really think why she was being so uptight, and she edged herself forward on the seat and smoothed down the silky skirt she was wearing and looked covertly at the man beside her—his handsome, forceful profile, the straight line of his brow, the enigmatic mouth, Suddenly she felt a shiver deep within her. Her cattleman! 'Exactly what you're looking for, Edie,' Barb had said. 'A man who wants to get married.'

She moved uneasily and asked him in a small voice, 'Is it a good hotel?'

'The best,' he assured her solemnly . . .

Some five minutes later Edie—Mrs Drew Sutton according to the hotel register—was standing in the middle of the hotel bedroom looking, with a sickening sensation in the pit of her stomach, at the double bed that dominated the room. Drew was busy adjusting the curtains or the windows—she didn't know which and didn't care—and by the time he'd turned towards her again she'd more or less composed her reeling senses and was able to ask him chillingly, 'Is this a joke? If so, I find it in very bad taste.'

'A joke?' he repeated. 'What do you mean?'

She bit her lip. 'The—bed. You could at least have asked for twin beds.'

He looked at her steadily for several seconds, then stooped to pick up her suitcase and fling it on to the end of the bed. 'What man has twin beds on his wedding night?' he asked grimly. 'No, it's not a joke, Edie. I've already told you, for me it's dead serious. As for the damned bed—whatever its size it's not going to make any difference to our relationship. If it'll make you happy, I'll sleep on the floor. It won't be any hardship—I've slept outside on the ground half my life, you know—a soft and downy bed is not something I can't do without.'

He opened her suitcase as he spoke, and she moved forward embarrassedly to get her toilet things. Being married to Drew Sutton was going to be even more difficult than she had imagined. She'd vaguely pictured their lives barely touching—separate rooms, closed

doors, politeness. Why, she didn't really know. Instead
there were going to be dangerous intimacies, moments
when she would wish she could quite simply disappear
through a hole in the ground. This was one of them.

She almost snatched her things from the open suitcase, and turned towards the bathroom. A moment
later she was locked in there alone, aware of every
quivering nerve in her body. The thought of him sleeping on the floor disturbed her, which was absurd. As
she splashed her face at the basin she caught a glimpse
of her brand new wedding ring—a plain wide band of
yellow gold—and a rush of tears came to her eyes.
'Fool!' she told herself with a touch of hysteria as she
wiped her eyes furiously on the hotel towel.

When she went back into the room Drew was hanging his clothes in the wardrobe with a composure that
made nonsense of her hysteria, and without speaking to
him, she sat down in front of the mirror.

She was brushing on eye-shadow when she became
aware that he was watching her and she paused and
stared back at him, her eyes wide and a little frightened.

'I don't know why you bother with all that stuff,' he
remarked, coming closer. 'Your eyes don't need it.
They're your most beautiful feature, you know that?—
and that's *really* saying something.'

Edie's heart gave an unexpected and treacherous
thump, but she managed a derisive smile.

'I wish you wouldn't mess around trying to flatter
me. It's quite pointless. I'd far sooner you went downstairs to the bar or somewhere and waited for me
there. I've used eye make-up for years and I like it,
so——'

'So I'm to shut up? All right, all right, do as you
please. God knows it will never do to quarrel on our

wedding day,' he said sardonically.

A minute later the door closed behind him and she was alone.

She took her time before she went downstairs to the lounge to join him.

They spoke to each other very little over their pre-dinner drinks, but the alcohol gave her at least a slight feeling that nothing mattered as much as she had thought, and by the time they went in to dinner she was more able to cope with the situation.

After dinner, they took a walk in the town. This inland city was as unlike Sydney—two and a half thousand kilometres away—as it could possibly be, and Edie was deeply aware of its isolation as she looked up at the sky bright with stars, and felt the warmth of the air flowing in from the vast plains and the desert scrublands. Drew talked pleasantly and impersonally, telling her that the mining of silver, lead, zinc and copper were responsible for the existence of this city, set in a district that was otherwise given over to the growing of beef cattle. They were facts that Edie had known before with her head only, but now, strolling along with Drew, she realised them on a different level, and had at the same time a strong sense of having cut herself off from a very distant past. All by rushing off quite crazily into the unknown to marry someone of whom she knew nothing.

But the strangest thing of all was that she had actually married him. And when Drew stopped to speak to a couple of men, casually introducing her as his wife, she looked at the newcomers through her lashes. They were both cattlemen, but very different from Drew, their faces so weatherbeaten it was hard to guess their ages. She could have found herself married to a man like one of them, she thought. But now—she knew she could not have faced it. As it was, she was married, and yet not married, to a man who appeared to belong to two worlds. At their first encounter, she had found nothing remotely resembling the cattleman about him. Since then—since then she had caught more than a glimpse of the other side of his character—the toughness, the ruthlessness, the disregard for the conventions that doubtless came from living the life he did.

These thoughts ran swiftly through her mind like little currents criss-crossing in a stream as she stood apart, not even trying to listen to what he and the other two men were saying. But when he took her arm and they were on their own again, she felt something in her relax. Which was—funny.

Back at the hotel he paused in the foyer to tell her, 'Go on upstairs and get to bed, Alfreda. You look tired out. I shan't be up till later.'

She met his eyes. 'Drew——' she began hesitantly.
'What?'

She moved closer to him and spoke in a low voice though no one was about. 'You—you don't have to sleep on the floor. It's—a big bed.'

He gave her a slant-eyed look but said nothing, and after a second she turned and ran up the stairs, hoping desperately that he hadn't misunderstood her, and not sure why she'd said what she had. Except that it didn't seem fair——

Her pyjamas were short ones, white and sleeveless, with pink binding at the neck and the armholes. She'd never worn nightgowns and somehow she was glad of that tonight. She knew that lots of men slept naked and it was reassuring to see a pair of dark blue pyjamas on the chest. Belonging to Drew Sutton. Her—her husband.

She got into bed but left his reading light burning—

the one on the side nearest the door. She lay quite still for a moment, listening, then drew her left arm out from under the sheet and looked at the gold band on her finger. Her wedding ring. A ring that meant nothing—even though she had to share this room with a man tonight. And what about other nights? she wondered worriedly. At Dhoora Dhoora, would she sleep in the room she'd occupied before? Would it matter to Drew what Mrs Wilson might think? An image of his face floated into her mind—not only his face, but the whole of him. The broad shoulders, the narrow hips—his brown, long-fingered hands, whose strength she knew. They had been dusty yesterday, rough against her skin. She remembered with a burning intensity the way he had kissed her, and she could hear his voice saying, 'The way I feel right now I'm not inclined to wait.'

Oh God! She moved restlessly under the sheet as the shaming realisation came to her that the memory of it all was stirring those desires in her body that he had wakened when he'd held her the way he had, kissed her the way he had. She edged further over to her own side of the bed and wished she hadn't said he needn't sleep on the floor. Heaven knew what he had made of that. She knew his strength now, and worse, she knew her own weakness. 'It can't go on,' she thought on the verge of panic. At Dhoora Dhoora she would flatly refuse to share a room with him no matter who had to be convinced their marriage was a real one. To do so, night after night, would be impossible and quite unnecessary. 'If only——' she thought, but her conscious mind stopped there. If only what—she didn't know.

It must have been very late before he came into the room, for she didn't hear him, although she had lain awake so long she thought sleep would never come.

When she woke, it was light and she turned cautiously
to discover that she was alone in the bed. On the floor,
Drew Sutton was stretched out asleep. He wore
pyjama pants, but his torso was naked and she could
see the mat of golden brown hair on his chest. There
was no pillow under his head and his smoky brown hair
made a wave across his forehead and the line of his
lips was relaxed and strangely softened.

Propped up on her elbow, Edie stared at him for a
long time. It caused her an odd feeling of shame that
he had slept all night on the floor, uncovered, with no
mattress. Their wedding night. But it wasn't that sort
of a wedding, she reminded herself impatiently.

She slipped out of bed, quietly gathered up some
clothes, then shut herself up in the bathroom to shower
and dress. Before she came back into the bedroom she
stood with her hand on the door handle, listening. Was
he awake? She hated the thought of bursting in on him
unawares, yet to knock seemed absurd, and finally she
opened the door.

He was standing by the window in his pyjama pants,
and his grey eyes looked across at her with a quizzical
laziness.

'You're dressed,' he said amusedly, and she caught
her lip between her teeth. It was almost as if he had
accused her of doing something she shouldn't have
done—or something prudish.

'Yes,' she said coolly. 'The bathroom's all yours. I—
I hope you didn't have a bad night,' she added after a
second. 'You didn't have to sleep on the floor, you
know.'

'No?' His glance slid over her, from her face to her
feet, still bare. 'I wasn't quite sure what your—invitation meant, so I thought I'd better be on the safe
side. I probably slept better on the floor, anyhow.'

'What do you mean?'

'What do you think I mean? Do you imagine if I'd been lying inches away from a girl with your attractions —in a big comfortable bed at that—I'd simply have closed my eyes and fallen asleep? I wouldn't, you know——'

'You should have booked separate rooms for us,' she said, her cheeks scarlet. 'Or—or we could have gone straight back to Dhoora Dhoora.'

'Ah—the haven of Dhoora Dhoora,' he said mockingly, slinging a bathtowel over one tanned shoulder. His pyjama pants hung low on his hips and she raised her eyes, embarrassed, from the line of darkish hair that ran down the centre of his abdomen from below his navel. 'You feel you'll be quite safe there, do you?'

'I—I ought to be.' She tried to keep her voice cool and even. 'After all, it was you who set out the conditions for our marriage, Mr Sutton—though they weren't exactly what you implied in your advertisement.'

He came close to her and put his fingers under her chin, tilting her face up roughly to compel her to look at him.

'Do you feel like changing the conditions, Edie?' he asked, his voice harsh.

She jerked away from him as though his touch—or his words—had burnt her. Change the conditions, just because he found it hard to keep his hands off her!— just so he could—sleep with her!

'The conditions suit me perfectly,' she flung at him. 'I realise I made a silly mistake in coming here at all, but I'll—I'll help you out, and then I'll go ... Are you coming down to breakfast soon? I'm hungry——'

'I'll be ready in minutes,' he said, unmoved.

He went into the bathroom but he didn't close the

door. Edie put on her sandals, folded her clothes away, packed up her bag. She could hear the sound of the shower, and then his voice called, 'Alfreda!'

Her heart jumped. Did he think she'd gone down to breakfast without him?

'I'm still here,' she said clearly. 'I'm packing up.'

'I know you're still there. I was wondering if you'd like to come out to the muster with me when we get back home.'

'What?' She had heard him perfectly but she'd been taken by surprise.

He said something else and this time she didn't catch it, and she said, 'What?' again.

'For God's sake, if you can't hear me, come to the door ... I asked how you'd feel about camping out for a couple of nights.'

Camping out—with the stockmen. Drew had turned the shower off and she stood where she was, in front of her open suitcase. She wasn't at all sure she'd like camping out with the stockmen, but couldn't it be better than the alternative?—staying alone in the house all day, being alone in the house at night with him—— She turned, her mouth half open, ready to ask exactly what he meant, and discovered he had come into the bedroom, a towel around his hips, his body and hair still wet, and the sight of him so disconcerted her she forgot what she was going to say. She glanced away from him uneasily and he exclaimed impatiently, 'Well? Did you hear what I asked you?'

'Yes, I heard——'

'Then?'

'I was—I was thinking about it. Did you mean—camping out with the men?'

'Sure I did.'

'And if I—don't camp out, will you?'

'No, of course not. I can't leave you at the homestead on your own all night. Not when we're just married,' he concluded sardonically.

She bit her lip. 'Then I'll camp out.'

'Great. That suits me,' he said almost grimly. He took a minute to gather up his clothes, then disappeared into the bathroom again.

CHAPTER FOUR

THEY were back at Dhoora Dhoora by late afternoon. The business of getting there had kept them on a nicely practical level as far as Edie was concerned, and by the time they reached Narrunga, where Drew had left his car, she was feeling desperately tired. It was a tiredness more emotional than physical, and yet it drained her as effectively as anything could have done, so that on the long drive to the station she was satisfied to sit back in a semi-conscious state, neither talking nor worrying.

Mrs Wilson's welcome at the homestead shocked her into full and uneasy consciousness. There were flowers everywhere and she had prepared a special celebration dinner that included wine—the latter possibly on Drew's instructions, Edie realised. Over dinner he raised his wine glass to Edie and toasted her—'To you, Mrs Sutton'—as he looked across the candlelight straight into her eyes.

Her glass halfway to her lips, she asked him coldly,

'Do we have to keep this up even when we're alone?'

The half smile in his eyes vanished instantly. 'Tell me the way you want it,' he said equally coldly, 'and I'll do my best to comply.'

Edie was silent, twisting and turning the long-stemmed glass, half closing her eyes and seeing it sparkle like crystals through the tangle of her long lashes.

'Well?' he persisted relentlessly.

How did she want it? She hadn't yet given herself sufficient time to think that out. But she did know that she felt suspicious of him—wary.

'You might try taking the situation in good part, at least,' he said, 'seeing you got yourself into it. Forget whatever it is that's turned you sour on the deal—my duplicity, or however it is you think of my tactics for getting myself a wife. I did give you a chance to renege, you might remember—and you didn't take it, did you? I don't really know why not, if you're determined on being hard to get on with now.' He paused, and she thought he was talking sense, yet she resented having him do so in that particular way. Besides, she couldn't look at things as dispassionately as he seemed to. What girl could, with a man so handsome and virile sitting opposite her at a candlelit dinner table? How could she help suspecting deep in her heart that if she started being too friendly, he might take advantage of it? And when she began to think that way, she was brought back to the absurd realisation that she had come here, of her own volition, to marry a stranger.

He, of course, had had no such intentions.

She stirred uneasily and told him, 'I—I don't mean to be hard to get on with.'

'You don't? You're going to get into the spirit of the game?'

She tried to smile and wished she didn't find it so enticing to look into his grey eyes and try to read what was going on in his head. She wished too that she didn't feel that undeniable shiver of physical pleasure every time her glance rested on the strong curving line of his lips, the fall of hair across his very masculine forehead. If only he could have been the lean, rangy cattleman she had conjured up in her mind before she came here, she wouldn't be so disconcerted. She could have *dealt* with a lean rangy cattleman. Though she was far from sure that she'd have married him ...

Drew was tackling his dinner, but raised his head to advise, 'I suggest we come to terms—make the best of it, anyhow.'

What did that mean? Edie wondered cynically. If she were pleasant, friendly, heaven knew where it would all end. The fact was, she had taken his name, given him legal rights, and she was in a very physical way completely at his mercy. Physical superiority was probably a thing a man took very much for granted, and he wouldn't know how it could intimidate a girl who had only her guile to use when it came to fighting back. And Edie was far from sure she had enough guile to deal with Drew Sutton.

She raised her eyes and said unevenly, 'I'm prepared to make the best of it according to our agreement.'

His eyebrows rose. 'I wouldn't dream of suggesting anything else. But I take it you're still happy about coming out to the camp with me tomorrow?'

Yes, she was still happy about that, though it wasn't quite the way she would have put it herself.

'Then eat up,' he said with a tone of finality. 'You'll have to get yourself a good night's sleep. We'll be leaving at first light in the morning.'

Edie nodded. She tried to enjoy the chicken and its

delectable sauce that Mrs Wilson had evidently gone
to some trouble to prepare. It was followed by fresh
fruit salad and cream, and after that it was Drew who
made the coffee, telling her as he handed her a cup,
'Don't drink too much and keep yourself awake! You'd
better get your gear ready before you go to bed—jeans,
shirts, a change of underwear—a swimming costume if
you like. Bundle it all up and give it to me in the morning and I'll shove it in with the bedding.'

'Shall we—shall I be sleeping in a tent?' she asked.

'Sure you will, you'll be really pampered, seeing it's
your honeymoon,' he said lightly.

She smiled, but she wasn't really amused, and she
drank her coffee down thinking that Barb was probably
wondering what was happening to her in western
Queensland. Her eyes would fall out of her head if she
knew—but somehow Edie didn't think she was going
to give her the facts. She'd have to write, she supposed,
but she hadn't the least idea what she was going to
say . . .

'It's all quite crazy,' she wrote that night before she
got into bed, safe and secluded in the room where she
had slept before. 'I've married him, but don't worry,
it's not really a marriage at all.' She stopped and
chewed at the end of her pen, caught the elusive perfume of roses drifting in from the garden and felt suddenly too languorous to go on writing—elaborating on
this mad tale that Barb would find quite unbelievable
anyhow. What was the use of writing a letter in any
case? She had no idea when she could post it, particularly as they were going out to the muster camp tomorrow.

Edie Asher going out to the muster camp, she
mused. Sleeping out. Because of this—this man in her
life.

Suddenly she became aware of the silence, of the fact that there were only two people in this big house in the outback—herself and Drew Sutton, her—husband. She got up restlessly from her chair. The letter to Barb would have to wait. She stood listening, something in her urging her to leave her room, to look for Drew. But why? Was it because the silence was unnerving? Or was there another reason?

She didn't go and look for him. Instead, she crossed the room and locked the door. Then she undressed slowly, conscious as she had never been before of her virginal white skin, her untouched breasts. Remembering without willing it the way Drew's eyes looked at her, the feel of his hard body against her own. And then, as she got into bed, she thought of him—last night—sleeping on the floor beside her bed. The thumb of her left hand rubbed against the ring he had given her, the ring that had made her Mrs Drew Sutton.

'Do you feel like changing the conditions, Edie?' he had asked her.

'No,' she heard herself say aloud, and she added beneath her breath, 'It's just that I'm—feeling lonely.'

He woke her in the morning before it was light. He had made tea, cooked steak and eggs and toast, and they breakfasted together in the kitchen with the electric light burning. By sun-up they were in the Land Rover, travelling along the track away from the homestead.

Edie leaned back in the seat feeling a sense of almost unwilling pleasure and excitement. Drew was right; she should make the best of it. This, for instance, would be something to remember when it was all over and she was back in Sydney with Barb, nursing her old people again.

Drew wore a black shirt, black pants, and her eyes

went again and again to his long brown hands on the
wheel of the car, and then to his profile, which she was
beginning to know by heart. The sky had lightened,
galahs showed rose-coloured breasts as they rose in
great flocks to swim through the clear early morning
air. The paddock fences were squared in sharply
against the growing brilliance of the sky on the flat
horizons, and she saw a lone emu moving, unhurried,
confident, its big, feathered body oddly turtle-shaped,
its legs and head half hidden in the long grasses as it
stopped to feed. Clouds were lifting high into the sky
above the edge of the world to make a floating pattern
above, and silvery shafts of sunlight merged with the
soft golden haze on the eastern horizon. Everything
was new and beautiful and clean and unknown, and
deep within her Edie felt a sort of hunger stirring. This
could be a wonderful world.

Half an hour later, the day had lost its dewy fresh-
ness, its magic air of mystery and unreality. The air
was growing hot and breathless, and they had driven
into harsh scrubby country. As they came through the
mulga a while later, everything seemed suddenly to be
obscured by clouds of red dust. Across the plain that
opened out ahead of them there were horses and men,
jostling cattle, the rough rails of holding yards, while
closer at hand under the trees, a scattering of gear and
canvas proclaimed that they were at the muster camp.

Drew braked and turned to look at Edie for what
seemed the first time in hours, his grey eyes assessing,
enquiring. She blinked, trying quickly to veil her instant reaction, which had been one of slight shock.
How could she possibly put in days and days—and
worse still, nights and nights—out here in these primitive conditions? Water glinted through the trees, and
in the shade of some big trees a man, evidently the

camp cook, was making preparations for a meal. A whip cracked, a stream of cattle came reluctantly across to the yards in a cloud of dust, and Edie clenched her teeth.

'Sorry you came?'

Drew's eyes mocked her and she said instantly, 'Why should I be? It's—very interesting.'

'You reckon so?' He smiled lopsidedly. 'It's a pity you don't ride. When the novelty's worn off, you may find you're just a little bit bored.'

'Couldn't I learn to ride?' she retorted, and felt pleased at his look of surprise.

'I guess you could—if you're game.'

Well, she'd married a man like Drew Sutton. She should be game enough for anything.

Presently she had a mug of tea poured from a huge steaming billy, and as she drank she made the acquaintance of several laconic and quietly curious stockmen. Later, Drew set up a primitive tent for her away from those other rough shelters.

'Where will you sleep?' she asked him.

He shrugged and said drawlingly, 'Where I'll be expected to sleep—over here, with you.'

'*With* me?' she repeated.

'Near you,' he corrected himself dryly, and she coloured fiercely and changed the subject.

'When can I learn to ride?'

'You can have your first lesson in just five minutes. I'll have a quiet little horse saddled up for you. As quiet a horse as you can expect out here,' he added, his eyes glinting.

Edie felt a spasm of fear, but she didn't put a voice to it.

She had never been on a horse in her life and she was thankful that none of the men were around when a little later Drew helped her into the saddle. 'Put your left foot in the stirrup—now up you go——'

She looked at him helplessly and unexpectedly his hands went around her waist and he swung her up as if she weighed nothing. She felt herself miles above the ground on this 'little' horse, and her hands trembled as he put the reins into her hands and adjusted the stirrup leathers. In a frighteningly short time, she was riding at his side away from the yards and the camp, at first at a walk, but soon, as her horse followed his, at a trot. It wasn't difficult after all, although she was aware she hadn't fully adjusted to the rhythm of the horse's movements—and that later on she was going to feel very stiff and sore indeed. Drew gave her a few elementary lessons, and warned her against doing anything too drastic—'Pull too sharply on the reins and you're likely to be thrown, in your state of inexperience.'

She spent the rest of the morning in the saddle, though far from all of it with Drew. A good part of the time she merely sat her horse in the shade of the trees and watched the activity going on around her. She watched Drew in particular, naturally enough, and it was impossible not to be impressed at his performance on his tall black stallion.

Lunch was steaks and potato and bread, washed down by mugs of black tea. The men had some sort of boiled pudding, but not Edie, and it was a relief to her when Drew suggested she should spend the afternoon at the waterhole.

'That way you can keep cool and get yourself cleaned up in privacy as well—you're in a pretty dusty state and I reckon you've had enough riding for one day. Muscles feeling sore?'

'Not yet,' she said.

She didn't go straight to the waterhole after the men resumed work. She sat on the red earth, her back against a tree trunk, watching the cook cleaning up, watching the activity going on around the yards. The cattle were milling about, the dust was rising in clouds, and the ringers were continually bringing in more mobs. Most of all, as in the morning, she watched Drew on his black horse, with that long stockwhip of his. It was fascinating to watch him use it to pick out a beast from the yards—curling it with lightning speed through the air, using magic to bring a specific animal where he wanted it so it could be drafted into another yard. She could have watched for hours, she thought, and then discovered she was on the point of falling asleep. The only thing that kept her awake was the growing soreness in her muscles. A long hot soak in a bath would have been just the thing, but there was no bath here, no hot water, no shower even. Presently she got up stiffly from the ground and went back to the tent Drew had put up for her use. One side of it was completely open, and there were two bedding rolls on the ground—his and hers. She hadn't given him her gear but had packed it in a flight bag, and from there she took out her swimsuit and went rather nervously away from the camp towards the waterhole she'd seen earlier.

It was unexpectedly cool and shady there, with dry sparkling red sand all around and tea trees leaning over the water. Cockatoos, perched in eucalypts a little further off, shrieked occasionally, and lizards basked in the sun or moved slowly through the stiff grasses. Edie got quickly into her swimsuit and was soon in the water. It was sunwarmed and gentle and deep enough to swim, and she spent a long time there.

When she went back to the camp, the work was still

going monotonously on, and she sat in the Land Rover, because although it was hot, it was kinder to her aching muscles than sitting on the hard ground. Drew appeared to have forgotten her completely, for he never once glanced her way. For her part, her eyes, screwed up against the sun, followed his every movement, even though she felt more than a passing irritation with her own fascination. Drew Sutton at work. Her cattleman. Her husband.

She was stunned when later he rode straight over to the Land Rover as if he had known all the time that she was there, and leaned down from his horse to look at her.

'How goes it, Mrs Sutton?'

She felt her heart jump and an instant protest rose to her lips, but somehow she stifled it, and instead gave him a wry smile.

'I'm beginning to pay for my enthusiasm,' she told him.

'I'll give you a massage later,' he promised her, and her eyes widened. He sprang down on to the ground and holding the reins loosely in his hands leaned in at the open window. 'Isn't that the right treatment—seeing you can't indulge in a long hot soak, nurse?'

'Yes,' she said, embarrassed. 'But I can manage without your ministrations, thank you. I'll be all right tomorrow.'

'What's the matter? Are you afraid I don't know anything about muscles? You'll find I'm quite an expert at easing your aches and pains.'

She pressed her lips together. 'That's—that's not the point. I just don't happen to want you to—to massage me.'

'Oh, for God's sake, are you going to add coyness to your other foibles? You're in the bush now—there's no room for sensitivity and bashfulness.'

Her other foibles? What exactly was that supposed to mean? On the point of asking him, she changed her mind. She leaned across and opened the car door on the other side and climbed out.

'I'm going to see what the cook's doing,' she told him over her shoulder—and hoped he didn't notice how stiffly she walked as she made her way across to the truck.

The stockmen cleaned up before dinner. Some were more fastidious than others—and some were not fastidious at all, and Edie didn't blame them after the long and hard day's work. Drew was the only man present who managed to look immaculate, and she wondered if that was because he was the boss or if it was for her benefit, but she didn't ask him. Dinner was a rough and hearty meal, and she shared hers with Drew while the men lounged on the ground, eating and talking. The sky was dark and sparks leaped up from the camp fire. In the yards, the cattle were quiet, kept so by a couple of men on horseback who rode around them constantly. The other stock horses had been hobbled and would be rounded up in the morning by the horse tailer, Drew told her—before it was light, for work began then.

It was strangely dreamlike sitting in the open air with the darkness of the sky overhead, the Southern Cross bright, and the glow of the camp fire lighting the trees and the faces of the men. Edie felt really conscious for the first time of how vast a land this was—and of how small and lonely a group they were, out there on the plain. But she was tired, terribly tired, and it was a relief when Drew asked her, 'Do you feel like bed?'

She closed her eyes wearily. 'Oh, I do—I do!'

'Then run along. I'll be across in a few minutes to give you that massage.'

'*No!*' she protested vehemently.

'Yes,' he said implacably.

She had got awkwardly to her feet, all too aware of the tenderness of her muscles, and he'd got up too, and she looked up at him defiantly. The longing for a hot bath was almost intolerable, but all the same, she didn't want his attentions.

Yet why ever not? she asked herself a few minutes later when she had escaped from him to the darkness of her tent. The firelight didn't reach to here, and she stripped off her clothes as quickly as she was able and got into her pyjamas. It would be bliss—it would be heaven—to have her sore body massaged. And Drew claimed to be something of an expert.

She had unrolled her bedding when she became aware that he had come to the tent.

'Okay,' he said briskly. 'Lie down on your tummy.'

'It's—all right,' she faltered, and added firmly, 'I'm not being coy—I'd just rather get into bed and go to sleep.'

'Liar,' he said briefly, and she looked at him indignantly as he stood in the opening of the tent. It was impossible to read his expression, for the glow of the fire turned him into a dark silhouette. Faceless, he could have been any cattleman standing there. Or any other man in the world. But he wasn't any cattleman, and he wasn't any other man in the world. He was Drew Sutton, the man she had married yesterday. And she could feel a kind of warmth emanating from him. Strangely, it seemed not merely a physical warmth, but another sort of warmth as well—the warmth of a personality.

And when he reached out his hand and said softly,

cajolingly, 'Come on, Edie, be sensible——' she turned from him and flung herself down on her face as obediently as a child.

It was all the bliss she had imagined and more to have his strong firm fingers massaging her aching muscles. He pulled her pyjama jacket up and slid the elastic top of her pants down, and his fingers eased the muscles of her back, of her buttocks, of her thighs, his hands warm and confident and comforting on her flesh. She was almost asleep before he'd finished with her, barely conscious of his telling her to turn over, of his opening the bedding roll and covering her up.

'I'll be right along, Edie,' he said then, so close to her ear she knew she wasn't imagining the words.

After that, she drifted into a half waking dream—of Drew kissing her as she lay on the hard ground, his lips against her own, their bodies, close, intimate—— This was how it must have been for the pioneer women who came with their men to the untamed outback, accompanied them on their mustering trips—often of necessity, because there'd be no homestead, no comforts, only a rough home of wattle and clay with beaten earth for a floor, no windows. Those women had borne children, nurtured them, lived lonely lives until they died.

Edie shivered a little in her bedding roll. What would it be like to have the comfort of a man lying here beside her? Like nothing in this world—like nothing she had ever experienced before—just as Drew's kiss two nights ago had been an entirely new experience for her. She heard the soft lowing of the cattle, the whistling of a Willie Wagtail, the sad cry of a curlew, and her thoughts drifted back to the flat she had shared with Barb in a Sydney suburb; to the man who had come home with her, kissed her on the sofa, grabbed at her, groped for her; to how she had wriggled away in distaste and how they had never—not one of them— ever said 'Will you marry me?' Marriage was an old-fashioned thing. Sex came first, and your partner might be more or less permanent or he might not. How would that sort of thing go out here? she wondered, and it seemed to have no place.

She heard a movement and she knew Drew had come to the tent. In the darkness she watched him un-dress down to his shorts and stand for a moment against the distant dying glow of the camp fire—broad-chested, narrow-hipped, almost naked. He was her husband, and yet she would be outraged if he tried to get into bed with her, to make love to her here on the bare red earth. She turned on her side and pushed the thought forcibly from her mind.

'Edie?' She felt the warmth of his breath close to her cheek, and she moved sharply.

'What?'

'You aren't asleep. Are you afraid? Do you want me to come in beside you?'

She turned away from him with a swift movement and covered her head with the blanket.

'Let me alone,' she said huskily.

After that there was silence.

Her muscles were still sore next day despite the mass-age, and Edie decided against riding. In any case, after lunch the men were moving on to make another camp, and Edie watched the packing up. Some of the men had been detailed to walk the sale bullocks back to the yards where they would be trucked off for sale, and she watched the mob set off. The branding and de-sexing were over, and the yards were empty, all the canvas and other gear had been packed up, and finally another cavalcade set off, a cavalcade of men and horses, for each stockman had three horses to allow for resting, the cook had two, and there were six night horses as well as eight pack animals to carry the plant. Last to leave was the cook in the truck, and when he had gone there remained only Edie and Drew and the Land Rover.

Edie felt exhausted and she knew she looked exhausted. It was excruciatingly hot, her body ached and the thought of moving off to another camp and starting all over again had become almost too much to bear. Yet not for worlds would she have protested to Drew or told him how much she had begun already to miss the comfort of a hot shower, or the privacy of a civilised toilet. If she and Drew had been in love, it might have been completely different, but as it was, there just seemed too much to cope with altogether.

It was a shock as well as a relief when Drew, pausing to light a cigarette as he strolled across to the Land Rover, already loaded with Edie's tent and her flight bag, her bedding and his—looked across the flame of the match to ask her astutely, 'Well? Have you had enough? Or are you ready for more?'

She didn't answer straight away. For her pride's sake, she wanted to claim to be ready for more, but on the point of doing so, she paused. She wasn't ready for more, so why on earth should she subject herself to more? Why shouldn't she go back to the homestead and sleep in a comfortable bed and take a hot bath when she wanted it instead of roughing out here? Why should she suffer to save Drew from having to come back home each night? She didn't really care if he came back or not, she wasn't afraid, and if it was a matter of conscience—or appearances—for him, then that was his worry. After all, she was the one who was doing the favour.

So she told him flatly, 'I've had enough. When I go back to Sydney I'll be able to tell my patients just what it's like to rough it at a muster camp.' She looked straight at him, not even blinking in the brilliant sunlight. 'I'd like to go back to the homestead.'

He didn't comment and after a second she added, 'If that's going to make me a nuisance, I won't object if you take me in to Narrunga and leave me there to get back to civilisation.'

His grey eyes surveyed her narrowly, and then he shook his head. 'No, you're not going back to civilisation, Alfreda. Is it that, or is it your old boy-friend you're thinking of?'

Edie blinked. 'Joe?'

'Is that his name? Joe, then. He has more attractions to offer you than a cattleman after all, I suppose.'

Edie found she had to make quite an effort to concentrate on Joe—slim, fair-haired, good-looking, wrapped up in his own world, which was the world of advertising. She had wrestled with him—how long ago? it seemed an age!—on the sofa in the flat—— She glanced at Drew Sutton from under her lashes and felt a strange spasm in the region of her heart. Oh no, Joe didn't have more attractions to offer than a cattleman—than *this* cattleman. In fact, it didn't worry her one little bit that she'd most likely never see Joe again.

Meanwhile, she and Drew were looking at each other in the burning sunlight and she heard her own indrawn breath as she moved jerkily towards the Land Rover, opened the door and got in. He was beside her in seconds, but instead of starting the motor he put out his cigarette, stretched his arm along the back of the seat behind her shoulders and looked hard into her face.

'Well? You want to chicken out?'

'Suppose I do——'

'Then it's too bad for you.'

'You mean you wouldn't let me go? Isn't that rather —unfair? I've married you—you have a—a marriage certificate. What more do you want?'

He looked at her levelly and then said drawlingly, 'What would you say if I told you I wanted—you?'

Edie felt her pulses begin to pound. 'What do you mean? You—you said you didn't expect to find yourself a real wife this way——'

His mouth curved in a sardonic smile. 'It would be a chance in a million, wouldn't it? But you were a real surprise packet. Hardly the wacky little nurse I'd been expecting.' He raised a hand and his fingers trailed down her cheek, and she felt herself shiver. 'You're a stunner, Edie. You know that? You're as beautiful as the desert rose. Any man in my position would be tempted to take you for his wife in deed as well as in name.'

She bit her lip and gazed out past him at the burning red of the earth, the straw-coloured grass trampled by the cattle, the deserted yards where the dust was no longer stirred. She looked at the trees beneath which there was now nothing but shadows since the stockmen's gear had gone, and from them a flock of white cockatoos flew up suddenly into the cloudless blue of the sky. She felt devastatingly aware of the fact that she was alone with Drew Sutton whose eyes, when she returned to them, were on her face like a caress. A caress that lingered on her eyes, then slipped gently down to her bosom, its curves plainly revealed by the pink cotton knit vest she wore.

She turned her head away and said huskily, 'For heaven's sake, what kind of a wife do you think I'd make a—a cattleman? I—I hate it already out here at the muster camp—heat and dust and flies and—and no comforts——'

'Good God, do you think that bothers me?' he said amusedly. 'Do you think I'd expect any woman to follow me out here to the cattle? The pioneering days are over, my dear.'

'But the days of isolation aren't, are they?' she rejoined. 'It's lonely here—don't you even know that?'

'Sure I know it.' His eyes hardened. 'But when a woman has a home to look after, a man to come back to her at the end of the day, children, her life is full enough. Besides, we do have neighbours, you know— and ample room for house guests at Dhoora Dhoora.'

She raised her eyebrows, her colour heightened. 'Are you—are you trying to persuade me to become your— your lawful wedded wife, Drew?'

'You're the one who started talking about wives, Edie,' he said unfathomably. 'But if I did decide to persuade you into anything, believe me, it wouldn't be with words,' he concluded, and this time he did start the motor.

Five minutes later she asked him tautly, 'Where are you taking me?'

'To the homestead. That's what you want, isn't it?'

'But you—you have to go out to the muster.'

'I don't have to do a damned thing. I'm the boss here. I can please myself what I do. I'm taking you home, Edie, and I'm staying the night with you. No one's going to be surprised.'

She shivered at the way he said it. 'You—you don't have to stay at the homestead. I'd—I'd rather you didn't.'

She saw his lip curl. 'Now come on—you can't have it all your own way. I'm taking you home to please you, and to please myself I'm staying to keep you company.'

'But—but why?' She remembered too clearly what he had just said about persuading her. Did she want to be persuaded to become his wife? Was it really any different from deciding you'd marry someone who'd advertised for a wife? Yes, it was very different, she decided. Because this was real, and that other mad thing she'd done—she'd never have seen it through. Yet, she reminded herself bewilderedly, now she was Mrs Drew Sutton. He'd persuaded her as far as that already. But with words, with nothing else.

'Why?' she heard him say. 'So we can get on closer terms with each other, of course. Doesn't that make sense?'

Edie had no idea what to say. She didn't even know if he was serious or not.

CHAPTER FIVE

UNPACKING in her room some time later that day, Edie wondered not for the first time why she had let herself be persuaded to marry him. It seemed that, with one foolish action—answering that ad—she had set in train a whole chain of impossible events. Events that had no place in the life of Edie Asher, nurse. Now here she was more or less tied up intimately with a stranger—Drew Sutton.

She tried to counter his presence in the homestead with indifference, but found it an ineffectual weapon on the very first night they were there together.

That night after they'd eaten, Edie carried the dishes

out to the kitchen before joining him in the sitting room for the ritual of coffee. He had put a cassette on the recorder to provide soft background music, one lamp was lit and the long curtains had been pulled back from the open doors so that the cooler air of night flowed into the room, bringing with it the scent of roses. Romantic, was Edie's first thought, but Drew asked her over his coffee, 'Do you play chess?'

She shook her head, a little taken aback.

'Shall I teach you?'

'No, thank you,' she said, somehow not caring for the idea. 'I wouldn't be any good at it,' she added to excuse herself. 'I have no head for strategy. I'd rather just——'

'Just what?' he wanted to know, as she paused, uncertain as to what she had been going to say.

His silvery eyes were travelling over her insinuatingly, and she told him hastily, 'Just *talk*.'

'Fine,' he said with a faint smile.

Following that there was complete silence. Drew was leaving it up to her and she had no idea what to talk about. As well, she found it distinctly hard to think while he was leaning back in his chair looking at her the way he was.

'Did you live in this house as a child?' she asked him desperately at last.

He looked surprised. 'I thought I told you my father managed the outstation. I lived there till I was going on for seventeen. I'll take you over there one day. You'll like Damien and his wife Mickie. They're what you might call our nearest neighbours.'

Edie bit her lip. The idea of meeting neighbours—being introduced as his wife—having to act that way—was nerve-racking. Anyhow, 'one day' meant nothing, so she wasn't going to worry about it yet. She glanced

uneasily around the big room, and the soft lighting and
the romantic music disturbed her. She thought of all
those other empty rooms, and she asked, still tense,
'Surely your uncle didn't live here alone till you came!
He wasn't married, was he?'

'No. But of course he didn't live alone. He had a
housekeeper.' He leaned forward and set down his
coffee cup on the tray she had placed on a small table,
then still leaning forward, his legs apart, he lit a cigarette and looked at her narrowly through the smoke.
'When I was thirteen or so, and away at boarding
school, my aunt Anne and my cousin Greg, who was
then a kid of eight, came to live here. Four years later,
as I told you, I joined the household, and as well as that,
Laurel Clarkson, my aunt's goddaughter, spent a fair
bit of time with us. So you see, we were quite a family.'

'And it all broke up after your uncle died?' Edie relaxed a little and leaned back in her chair, her hands
behind her head. It seemed a pity a big house like this
should be so empty—and it hadn't been so in other
days. Suddenly aware that her posture had drawn
Drew's eyes to her bosom, she lowered her arms and
hunched herself forward over her knees. 'Your cousin
Greg—he's the one who'll inherit Dhoora Dhoora if
you're not married?'

He smiled slightly showing his white teeth and corrected her. 'Greg won't inherit Dhoora Dhoora, Edie.
Have you forgotten? I'm married—I have a wife.'

Disconcerted, she blushed deeply and said edgily,
'Well, it doesn't really seem fair to me. I mean, if he
lived here all that time—from when he was a little boy,
a lot younger than you. And after all, his mother was a
Sutton——'

'Not by birth. But true, Greg is a Sutton—our
fathers were twin brothers. After Anne was widowed,

she'd have liked to marry my uncle, and she came here with her son with exactly that in mind. She's a very ambitious woman, is Anne. However, it didn't happen.'

It was the way he spoke rather than the words he said that made Edie comment, 'You don't like her.'

He shrugged. 'I respect her—as I'd respect any businesswoman. Unlike you, she thrives on games of strategy. It takes a keen opponent to get the better of her, in fact.'

'You used to play chess with her?'

'I'm not talking about chess. I'm talking about a different kind of game.'

She didn't know what he meant and he didn't offer to explain, so after a moment she asked, 'Where does she live now—since you took over?'

One eyebrow rose. 'I hope you're not picturing me showing her the door ... She married again shortly after Uncle Philip's death—a man she'd known for some years. A horse breeder, and a friend of her first husband's, if it's of any interest to you.'

'What happened to the others?' Edie asked, ignoring this gibe and not caring if he thought her inquisitive. 'Greg—and your aunt's goddaughter?'

'Greg decided to leave Dhoora Dhoora—entirely of his own free will. At twenty-one, he wasn't what you'd call co-operative, and he hadn't reached the stage where he could be made responsible for running the outstation. And of course, at that time, it looked as if Dhoora Dhoora was as good as mine with my marriage coming up.'

He said no more, and Edie, still hunched forward over her knees, was suddenly sombre. His marriage. But Deborah had died—just days before the wedding, it seemed. Although it had happened probably nine years ago, she somehow felt it would be insensitive on her part to intrude on that part of his life. Drew had remained unmarried, and the logical explanation for that fact seemed to be that he hadn't got over the loss of his fiancée. She glanced at him covertly and said in a low voice, 'It must have been a bad time for you ... What did Greg do? Didn't he ever want to come back?'

'No. He'd never been strongly attached to Dhoora Dhoora. It was mainly my aunt who had her eye on it. She didn't manage to get herself married to Philip, but she's not the sort of woman who gives up easily ... As for what Greg's been doing during the past few years, I couldn't really tell you. He took some interest in his stepfather's business and I've a strong suspicion he did a bit of betting on the horses. Since I was unmarried, he had a good income from Dhoora Dhoora. As a matter of fact, up until lately he's made a habit of paying a visit here once or twice a year. Possibly, among other things, to check how I was doing in the matrimonial stakes.'

'Is—is he likely to come here at this time?' Edie asked, a faint alarm in her heart.

'I hardly think so. He's shot off to Ireland to visit his mother and stepfather. Brian inherited a bloodstock farm in Limerick about a year ago, and Greg wanted to have a look at it. I imagine the farm needs money putting into it, and that's one reason I more than suspect Dhoora Dhoora would be put on the market if it went to Greg.'

'I—I suppose you've let them know you're married,' she said uncomfortably.

'I haven't, as a matter of fact. After all, it's barely happened yet, has it?'

Edie crimsoned. 'But it has—happened. You surely won't wait till the eighteenth to let them know the station belongs to you?'

'I'll probably write to my solicitors next week,' he said shortly. 'After that, it's up to them. And these things always take time.' He added, with an abruptness that took her by surprise, 'Come and sit by me on the couch, Edie. You've had your fill of talking by now, surely, and it's unnerving to sit here looking at you across a space of five feet under the circumstances.'

She stopped herself just in time from asking, 'What circumstances?' because she suspected he was referring to the fact they were, supposedly, married. Instead, she parried the invitation by remarking, 'I'd better take the coffee tray out to the kitchen.'

She picked up her cup from the floor, then stood up and crossed to the low table near the couch, but before she could stoop to it, Drew rose abruptly, brushing against her arm so that she dropped her cup and saucer on the floor. She uttered an involuntary exclamation of annoyance, but before she could even see what damage she had done, her wrist was encircled by his fingers and he had pulled her against him.

'Come on now, Edie, haven't we played it civilised for long enough?' he muttered. 'You know damned well how I'm beginning to feel about you, don't you?'

His face was inches from hers and she stared up into his eyes as though mesmerised. He had captured both her wrists and he held them behind her back as savagely as if she had been threatening him some way. She tried frantically to escape, but managed only to move her head, and immediately felt the roughness of his jaw against her forehead.

'Let me go,' she breathed. 'You're hurting me!'

'Then keep still,' he ordered, and she felt his thumbs pressing even harder against the delicate bones of her wrists.

'We can't go on being strangers like this—it's not possible——'

'It's possible to me,' she said on a breath that hurt. 'I'd—I'd prefer it.'

'I don't believe that.'

'You'll have to,' she panted, and twisted again in his grasp. He released her for the fraction of a second, but only to grasp her by the upper arms, so that now her breast was crushed against him.

'I want you, Edie,' she heard him breathe, and then he cupped one hand against the back of her head and his face came down to hers. 'Give in, give in,' he murmured against her lips.

She had known this would happen. She had known all along that he'd use his superior male strength against her. And it was so undignified to struggle—to scratch and bite and kick. And besides—besides——She heard herself give a soft moan as his mouth covered hers, and with her breath now gone and her body drawn intimately against his, she had no choice but to submit as he pulled her down with him on the long couch where he had been sitting a moment ago.

The cassette music cut out, the room was suddenly quiet. Vaguely, she heard the far-off cry of a mopoke, but after that she was aware of nothing except that Drew's body was covering hers, and his mouth was demanding more and more response from her—a response that she was quite helplessly giving.

It wasn't until he began undoing the buttons of her cream silk blouse and whispering urgently against her hair, 'Come to bed, Edie! It's crazy to be messing about here'—that she forced herself to move away from him. He let her go, but not because he thought he'd lost out. On the contrary. Glancing at him, she was shocked by the heat of the desire she saw in his eyes. Her own body was trembling, and she was so keyed up it was beyond her for the moment to force herself to her feet.

She put her hands over her eyes and told him unevenly, 'You—you told me I might have to remind you of your promise——'

'To hell with promises,' he said softly but violently. 'Aren't feelings—human emotions—more important than promises? I want you, Edie—don't let's talk—don't let's run away from it. Come to bed.' He had got to his feet and now he leaned down and, as if she weighed nothing, lifted her in his arms. She felt his male strength encircle her, and an obliterating warmth invaded her body so that she longed weakly to feel his lips on her own again. And not in vain either, for his mouth was devouring hers as he carried her from the softly lit room along the hallway to her own bedroom.

'We're married,' she kept reminding herself drowningly.

Drew didn't switch the light on, but a warm radiance from the moon fell across the verandah and lessened the darkness inside. He pulled back the bedspread with a sweeping movement and deposited her on the mattress, and she lay there, her dark hair fanned out around her face, not moving, her heart beating fast, a sensual lethargy possessing her so that she was incapable of rational thought. As though she were deep in a dream, she watched him start to undress, and then, crazily, just as he unzipped his trousers, the quiet of the night was shattered.

Someone was banging on the front door and a man's voice was calling 'Drew!' repeatedly.

Edie's nerves revolted and her body felt as if it had been flung hard and violently against solid rock. Her heart thumped at the shock of the rude interruption.

'Hell and damnation!' she heard Drew mutter. 'It's

Frank—I'll have to bloody well go——'

In seconds he had melted from the room and she sat up, hugging her knees. Was this fate stepping in—giving her time to reassess? Because—because, she thought appalled, wasn't this exactly how single girls got pregnant—carried away by the emotion of the moment? It was all very well for her to have told herself that she and Drew were married, she had no guarantee *he'd* been thinking of it that way. For all she knew, he might be no different from other men who'd wanted to make love to her—men who weren't interested in marriage or permanence or fidelity, but only in possessing her body for their own pleasure.

She drew a deep shuddering breath, feeling her heartbeats slowing down to normal. She had wanted Drew to be her lover—she had wanted it more than anything. But for that interruption, it would have happened by now, there'd be no going back.

She looked at the luminous clock on the bedside table. What on earth could Frank Wilson want at this time of the night? Though, ludicrously, it was only just after half past nine. Her thoughts had stopped their dizzy circling and the clamouring in her body was subsiding and she became aware of the sound of voices. Then a wire door slammed, footsteps crunched across gravel—and the silence came back. Drew must have left the house with Frank. Why? Was it some emergency? She'd better get up, find out what was happening.

She switched on the reading lamp and went to the mirror, stared at her own flushed face and wide, guilt-filled eyes, and discovered her blouse was undone. She fastened the buttons with clumsy fingers, brushed her hair. Now what did she do? The room looked strange to her, like the room of some person she didn't know, and she thought with an inward gasp of disbelief of the man who had stood by her bed undressing only minutes ago, while she lay waiting for him. His shirt was still on the chair where he had flung it. Another few seconds and it would have been joined by his pants, and then——

Edie pulled up her thoughts in mad mid-gallop. How easy it had been for him to persuade her!—and it certainly hadn't been with words. Had it been deliberate? *He* hadn't been carried away as she had. Or—or had he?

The wire door banged again and Drew came into the room while she was still in the middle of her thoughts, and his eyes looked at her across the room enigmatically as he picked up his shirt and put it on, covering the nakedness of his chest.

'Mrs Wilson's crook, Edie. I don't know if it's appendicitis or gallstones, but it's bad. I'm going to call the flying doctor. Go over and see her, will you—and try to calm Frank down a bit. His mother died for lack of help when he was a kid—his father worked on a station in the Centre.'

'I'll talk to him,' said Edie, drawn suddenly out of her self-absorption into someone else's troubles. 'Will the doctor come tonight, Drew? Or——'

'Sure he'll come. This is an emergency. Frank can come out with me presently and we'll get some flares lit on the strip so the doc can get his plane down with the least possible trouble. It's a good hospital—they've got everything, so don't you worry. There's a torch in the kitchen,' he added over his shoulder as he left the room. 'On the dresser beside the bread bin——'

When Edie hurried out there were lights all along the verandah, but beyond the trees that sheltered the garden there was a wide dark stretch to be crossed before she reached the bungalow, its yellow lights shining in the darkness. She flashed the torch ahead of her, thankful for its beam.

Inside the house, Frank Wilson stood beside his wife's bed, his face so grey beneath its tan one would have thought he was the patient instead of Mrs Wilson, who managed a brave smile as Edie came in.

Edie explained brightly and cheerfully that she was a trained nurse, asked a few questions and made a quick examination. She reached the conclusion that Mrs Wilson was suffering from appendicitis, not from gall-stones, and that the sooner she could be taken to hospital the better. She told Frank confidently, as she carefully packed a bag for the sick woman, 'Your wife will be okay, Mr Wilson. You mustn't worry—all sorts of advances have been made in medicine since the days when appendicitis was a really serious matter. Drew will be along presently—he wants you to go out with him and get the flares lit for the flying doctor.'

Only a few minutes later, car lights swept across the window, and Drew was there, and presently Edie was alone with Mrs Wilson.

'I'm sorry this has happened just now,' the house-keeper apologised, her face twisted with pain. 'You aren't having much of a honeymoon, are you? I'd have liked to be here to look after you a little so you'd be free to enjoy yourself with Mr Sutton.'

Edie turned away to hide her crimson cheeks. 'It doesn't matter in the least,' she said, and added un-truthfully, 'We'll probably have a proper honeymoon later on, anyhow, when—when Drew is really free.'

After that, the time passed somehow. Mrs Wilson didn't want to talk much, and Edie did what she could to comfort and ease her. It was a relief when the men came back and a still greater relief when, some time later, the hum of a plane could be heard, and the two men carried Mrs Wilson out to the car. Edie wasn't needed, and she went wearily back to the homestead, feeling years had passed since last she was there. She heard the plane take off finally, and reflected that it was fortunate she and Drew had come home that afternoon —though no doubt, if he had had to, Frank would have managed things himself. He'd have had to! After a moment's thought, she went to the kitchen and put the kettle on to boil. The men would appreciate a cup of tea when they came in—particularly Frank.

The news that came over the transceiver for Dhoora Dhoora in the morning was good. Mrs Wilson had been operated on for appendicitis and everything was okay. Drew drove out to the muster camp a lot later than usual, and his smile at Edie before he left was enigmatic.

'Think you can manage to cook dinner for me to-night, Mrs Sutton?'

'Don't call me that,' she said crossly, altogether uncertain of her feelings. She was wearing a short housecoat over her pyjamas, having only wakened when she heard Drew moving about the house. Now he crossed the kitchen and taking hold of her shoulders, he looked down into her eyes so that she was reminded with a painful, shaming vividness of those mad moments last night when she had been in his arms.

'I'm afraid you *are* Mrs Sutton,' he said, and she veiled her eyes quickly with her lashes, her face crimsoning. She'd fallen asleep too quickly last night once she was back in bed to have thought any more about what had been happening between her and Drew before Frank interrupted them. She hadn't even had time to give a thought to the embarrassment of seeing him again this morning.

'Well, whether I'm Mrs Sutton or not,' she said with determined dryness, 'I'm sure I can manage dinner.' She pushed past the look in his eyes that suggested he might want to talk of other things besides dinner and added hopefully, 'Will Frank be eating with us?'

'Good God, no,' he said impatiently. 'He can look after himself. We'll be dining alone—just you and me. You'll have to see how you can make out with the girls this morning, by the way. See you don't let them wriggle out of anything you want them to do—not anything at all. Be firm.'

Edie nodded and told him with a confidence she didn't really feel, 'I'll get on fine, don't you worry.'

He looked down at her mouth, and the very expression in his eyes seemed to make her lips feel warm, and knowing they were trembling, she moistened them nervously with the tip of her tongue. He was going to kiss her goodbye—just as if she were really his wife. Did that mean that tonight he'd expect to take up where they left off last night? Well, she was going to have all day to think about that, she reminded herself, and found little comfort in the thought.

Drew bent his head and his kiss was brief but firm. It was more the look in his eyes as she met them at close quarters that she found unnerving. Those eyes that had been so sharp and silvery now were warm with a desire that had melted their ice, and she felt her pulses begin to race. She knew she wanted him to kiss her again, but differently—and she coloured furiously when he shook his head slowly and said with an amused quirk of his mouth, 'No, Edie—definitely no. I have work to do.'

Had he? Hadn't he said he was the boss and could please himself? she caught herself thinking as he flicked her cheek carelessly and left her. Perhaps he

didn't really want to stay with her today. Perhaps that
thing last night was merely something he turned on
because he was a man who needed sex and who knew
how to arouse a woman. Any woman. How to stir her
senses and weaken her resistance. She was thoroughly
convinced he knew all about the gentle art of persua-
sion.

It was an unsettling thought, but it lingered at the
back of her mind all day.

She had never looked in the other bedrooms in the
homestead before, but that morning, as she planned
work for the two housegirls, Ellen and Ruth, she
opened each door to see if the room within needed
cleaning. Besides her bedroom and Drew's room, there
were four others, and the girls were adamant that there
was no work to be done in any of them, but remembering Drew's advice, Edie insisted on seeing for herself.

'No, missus, that Greg's room—he bin gone long
time now.'

Edie ignored the protest and took a good look
around, then decided the room was immaculate and
she couldn't possibly ask that anything more should be
done. She moved on and pushed open the next door.

'No more use that room, 'less visitors come,' said
Ellen, her big teeth showing in a cheerful smile.

The third room too was a guest room, and as immaculate as the others, and Edie reflected that Mrs
Wilson was certainly a treasure, and advanced confidently to the last room. Ruth and Ellen covered their
mouths with their hands and giggled.

'That Laurel's room. Clean 'im maybe last week.'

Laurel's room! Edie's glance lingered on the spot-
less, prettily feminine room. Unlike the other rooms
that had a vacant look about them, it looked somehow
as if it had been occupied only recently, and she was

aware of a feeling of curiosity. Laurel—Laurel Clarkson, hadn't Drew called her? Anne's goddaughter, the one who used to spend a lot of time here while Drew's uncle was still alive. She had asked Drew about Greg, and about Laurel. But though he had told her Greg was now in Ireland, he had said nothing at all about Laurel, and she, remembering Deborah and thinking of the trauma it must have been for Drew when she died —she had forgotten.

Somehow troubled, she told the girls to clean the bathrooms, checked to see they were doing it properly, then busied herself tidying the linen cupboard. She noticed that many of the sheets and pillow slips, the big tablecloths and damask napkins, must have been here since the days when the house was lived in by a family.

Much later, after the girls had gone, she walked slowly through the house and once again looked in the empty silent bedrooms. At least, she looked in two of them—Greg's room first of all, not entirely empty of his personal belongings, for on top of a chest there were a few books with his name scrawled in the front. There was an old school photograph of a Rugby team too, and she presumed that Greg was one of their number. Quite definitely, it had been a man's room.

But it was Laurel's room she really wanted to see, and she stepped inside the door feeling guilty. A faint perfume hung in the air as if Laurel—or somebody— had been there recently, or had stayed there often. For a moment Edie wished she had asked the girls how long it was since Laurel had slept there, but she knew that she couldn't and wouldn't ask them—not tomorrow, not ever. Her dignity forbade it. And anyhow, why should she care—or even be interested? Yet she did care, and she was interested, and she moved

slowly into the room and stood on the fleecy cream
carpet looking around her—looking for secrets. Outside the long windows the vine-draped verandah lay in
shadow, with the sun high overhead, and beyond it the
garden was in brilliant sunshine. Who had chosen the
pretty floral bedspread, the pale green curtains that
exactly matched it? she wondered. It was a very
feminine room and its soft furnishings struck her as
being newer than those in the other bedrooms.

After a few seconds, as if compelled, she opened
the wardrobe and looked inside. With a feeling of faint
but deadly shock, she found clothes hanging there—a
green velvet cloak, long dresses—— She closed the
door abruptly, then almost tiptoed to the chest of
drawers that, backed by a triple mirror, obviously
served as a dressing table. She stared at her own reflection and saw that her cheeks were pale and her eyes
bright. What on earth was she doing here? Well, didn't
she have a right? Wasn't she—Drew Sutton's wife?
She bit her lip hard and pulled open one of the drawers.
Scent, a pot of face cream, a small enamelled jewel box.
At the other side of the divided drawer, neatly folded
scarves, a few handkerchiefs, and, half hidden under
them, a coloured photograph in a silver frame. She took
it up, her fingers trembling. Three faces looked back at
her—one of them Drew's. The others she didn't know,
and she stared at them intently. A man and a girl.

Debbie? she wondered, looking at the blonde hair,
the laughing mouth. The girl stood between the two
men, each of whom had an arm around her shoulders,
and she looked happy and confident. It was sad that she
had died so young.

But it couldn't be Debbie, Edie realised suddenly.
Debbie had died nine or ten years ago and the Drew
in the photograph was the mature man she knew. So

was it Laurel? And the other man—handsome, smiling, a little arrogant—it must be Greg, she decided for no real reason whatsoever.

Had Laurel been in love with Greg? Or had she been in love with Drew?

It struck her after a moment that she was acting like a jealous wife, which was crazy. In all probability Laurel Clarkson was a kind of sister to the two men she had known since she was little more than a child.

Edie discovered she was looking at Drew's face, and she felt a shiver run through her bones. Tonight he would be coming home to her. And after last night, what was he going to expect of her? What was going to happen? Had they been a normal newly married couple they'd have made love.

But they weren't a normal married couple, and he was—yes, he was a stranger still. She knew next to nothing about him. With an impatient nervous movement she put the photograph back in the drawer where she had found it and slammed the drawer shut. She told herself she'd ask Drew again about Laurel tonight —and this time he'd have to answer her.

CHAPTER SIX

But she didn't ask Drew that night. She found she simply couldn't.

As she cooked dinner for two—braised steak with vegetables, to be followed by caramel cream—she thought of his saying, 'You'd be quite happy living here with your man coming home to you at the end of the day'. But when he did come, when she heard the sound of the car, she made a point of staying where she was, in the middle of something very important in the kitchen. He wasn't her man, so she didn't go to the verandah to greet him, and it was he who had to seek her out.

'Have a good day?' he asked from the doorway, and she felt a current run electrically along her nerves—because it could all have been so different.

'Did you?' she countered with a cool smile, instead of answering.

'Sure.' A brief pause, and she stooped to lift the casserole from the oven. As she rose he said from close behind her, 'I won't kiss you. I'm filthy—and you don't like that, do you? I've time for a shower, I hope, before you put that mouthwatering dish on the table.'

'Of course,' she agreed, and despite herself she turned to look at him, remembering too clearly how she had reacted before to his dusty unshaven state. She felt a shock go through her as she encountered his grey eyes, brilliant against the tan of his face, now coated lightly but definitely with red dust. He was badly in need of a shave too, and she turned away sharply. She had an almost physical sensation of the roughness of his jaw against her cheek, of those lips moulding themselves against her own in the most intimate possible way. She thought of her own breast being crushed against that partly unbuttoned sweat-stained shirt and she felt her most secret nerve centres respond in a way that was totally primitive and almost frightening.

He didn't touch her. After a second he walked out of the kitchen and she took several deep breaths to steady herself before she resumed what she had been doing.

They were so restrained over dinner they could have been two people who hadn't seen each other since childhood and couldn't fill the gap. Or so it seemed to Edie. She trembled to think what was going to happen afterwards. Though part of her mind was obsessed with thoughts of the faintly perfumed room she had entered that day, the photograph she had seen, she could find no casual way to refer to it or to Laurel. The nearest approach she made was to remark on the extra bedrooms.

'The girls said the—the empty ones don't need cleaning every day,' she said awkwardly. 'I suppose they're not much used.'

'That's right,' said Drew without much interest. 'We do get a bit of dust in the house when it's dry, but the housekeeper has an eye on that.' After that he changed the subject.

At the end of the meal he suggested they should take coffee on the verandah, where it was cooler, and when Edie brought it out she was at once aware of the perfume of roses.

Drew stood with his back to the rail, his face illumined by the small table lamp he had switched on and around which a few small moths that had somehow found their way in were already flying.

'Do you dance, Edie?' he asked, his voice cool and casual, as she set the coffee tray down on a table near the lounger.

'Yes.' She straightened up and looked at him in surprise.

'How would it appeal to you if I suggested we put some music on the player and danced, then?'

'I—I—don't you want to teach me to play chess?' she stammered.

'No,' he said uncompromisingly. 'We managed very

well without chess last night, didn't we—up until the time we had that rather untimely interruption.'

She turned away full of confusion, her cheeks burning. She hadn't the least idea what she wanted—or she told herself she hadn't, but she shivered when Drew said softly from behind her, 'You're going to sleep in my bed tonight, aren't you, Edie?'

As he spoke he put his arms around her and cupped her breasts in his hands so that her shiver deepened to one that was half delight, half fear.

'It—it wasn't the arrangement,' she heard herself protest almost inaudibly.

'I know it wasn't the arrangement.' His fingers were caressing her, and she closed her eyes and let him pull her back against his body, feeling a terrible weakness in her limbs. 'But you wanted it last night, didn't you?'

His words had an odd effect on her. Yes, she had wanted it last night—she had wanted it badly, because he had been so cleverly persuasive. Just as he was being cleverly persuasive now. His touch sent little impulses of pleasure along her nerves. It was very obvious he was no stranger to lovemaking. There must have been other girls since Deborah Webster, she thought —girls he had made love to even if he hadn't wanted to marry them. Now he was married to her, Edie Asher— but only because he had to have some sort of a wife by the time he was thirty-five. As far as she was concerned, she thought, he might as well have shut his eyes and stuck a pin in a list of names—that was the care with which *she* had been chosen. It was to be a marriage in name only, he had told her very positively. Now, because he was a virile, very masculine type of man, he wanted to make love to her—and God in heaven! she wanted to let him!

By now he had slipped down the narrow straps of

her dress, and his fingers were on her bare skin and she was too stirred to pull away. Why stop him—why not let him go on? she asked herself, her thoughts blurring. They were married—legally married. They—they didn't *have* to part as soon as the marriage had served its purpose. He—he wanted a wife—a family. Yet going to bed with him was no guarantee they wouldn't part. The arrangement was that he'd give her a suitable monetary reward when she'd fulfilled her contract— and if it was generous enough, he just might feel it covered certain things that hadn't initially been included in that contract.

Of course, he'd make sure she didn't get pregnant, she found herself thinking insanely.

He twisted her round gently and held her close against him, then bending his head he began kissing her, long and deliciously and drowningly, and she stopped thinking altogether. The passion of his kiss spread through her body like the green tendrils of a swiftly growing vine, and all her nerves leapt to life and some sensual yet mystic communication seemed to pass from him to her. Edie wanted him never to let her go. All she wanted in life was that he should gather her closer and closer and carry her away to some bed of roses ...

A second later, he pulled her down on the lounger and she could hear the cane squeaking and groaning as it received their weight. For a long moment, she was crushed beneath his body while his kiss went on and his hands caressingly explored her bare skin.

She had just dimly become aware of the disturbing fact that something hard was pressing against her shoulder blade when Drew lifted his mouth from hers and raising his body away from hers, set his feet on the floor. He straightened himself and stood upright, his hands on his lean hips, his hair dishevelled. She saw the flash of his teeth as he laughed deep in his throat and remarked, 'Oh God, Edie, here we go again! I can't make love to you like this—it's hopeless, really hopeless. Come to bed.'

She lay looking up at him, disturbed by his laughter, by his withdrawal, by his ability to break into their lovemaking this way—when she would have gone on oblivious, even though she'd become aware of physical discomfort.

He reached out a hand to her, but she didn't take it. She slipped the straps of her dress back into place and pulled her skirt down over her knees, sitting up as she did so. How much of a fool was he making of her? And how weak was she being to want him to make love to her when he hadn't gone back on his assertion it was to be a short-term marriage?

Half of her—more than half of her—didn't care, but with her head lowered she told him huskily, 'I'm—going to drink my coffee. And you said—you said we'd dance.'

There was a little silence, and she glanced quickly up at him and saw a nerve move in his jaw.

'I'm sorry, I guess I've been too precipitate. I was forgetting I have to woo you—even if we are married ... We'll have our coffee—and we'll dance, if that's how you want it.'

He vanished into the sitting room and she pushed back her long dark hair and got up dazedly to reach for her coffee. She heard the music begin, but it was a couple more minutes before Drew came back with two tiny glasses and a squat bottle.

'I hope the coffee's not cold. I thought you might like a liqueur with it.'

'Yes, I'd like that.' Edie tried to sound poised and at her ease, but she felt desperately uncertain of herself and she almost jumped out of her skin when he asked her conversationally, as he handed her one of the glasses that he'd filled, 'You've slept with a man before, of course, Edie?'

She had taken a large sip of the liqueur brandy and she almost choked on it. 'No, I—I haven't,' she said, avoiding his eyes. She knew her answer was not the one he'd expected, for she could feel him staring at her.

'Good God,' he said slowly at last. 'Is that the truth? You really haven't? You're not telling me that in case I'm shocked or disappointed or something?'

She shook her head and swallowed hard. 'I—never wanted to——' She stopped. She wasn't used to talking about this sort of thing, and the eyes she raised to his were unconsciously wide and innocent.

'You wanted to last night, didn't you?' he said softly. 'You wanted to five minutes ago. Why, Edie?'

Why? Edie's head swam. How could she tell him why when she didn't know why herself?—except that he had somehow made her want him. She couldn't even ask him why *he* had done *that*. She looked at him dumbly and took another mouthful of the liqueur. Their eyes held as he drained first his coffee cup and then his glass. He held out his arms to her.

'Well, never mind ... Shall we dance?'

She hesitated, then with a feeling of helplessness let him pull her into his arms.

He held her close against him and bent his cheek to her hair as they danced, but she knew she was waiting for something more, that her body was hungry for his touch. The liqueur had gone to her head and she was unsteady enough on her feet to have to cling to him, so that she was dizzyingly aware of the warmth of his body, the scent of his aftershave lotion, the talc he used ...

It was a shock to discover the music had ended and that Drew was releasing her.

Drew looked down at her and said with a smile that was almost formal, 'That was delightful.'

Had it been? Edie stared at him—questioningly, half expectantly.

He made a slight movement towards her, then his hand fell to his side, and his mouth and eyes were serious as he told her, 'I think it's time you went off to bed.'

'You', he had said. So he meant she was to go—alone. She felt a blind flash of hatred for him. It was like a slap in the face—a snub. Why? she wanted to ask. *Why?* But in a low voice, she wished him good-night and walked away, feeling herself just a little off balance.

In her room she lay on the bed and wept out her frustration and hated herself instead of him. Because she shouldn't feel this way. But why had he changed? *Why?* She said the words aloud, thumping her pillow futilely. Because she was a virgin? And if it *was* because of that, then it was obvious it hadn't even occurred to him that they might make their marriage a real one—one that would last way beyond the time covered by the terms of their contract.

She, Edie Asher—no, Edie *Sutton*—she'd have been willing to make it a real marriage. She'd fought against the thought, but she was ready to admit to it now. Though only to herself.

In the morning Drew told her, 'We're going over to the outstation today. Damien contacted me over the transceiver—he wants my opinion on some problem he has.'

'You—you go,' Edie told him shakily, her eyes

darkly shadowed from a troubled night. 'You don't have to take me along.'

'I damned well do,' he said, his voice suddenly hard. 'Dame and Mickie know about my marriage. They want to meet you and I want them to meet you.'

She didn't believe him. There was no reason why he should want his friends to meet her. Besides, she wasn't ready to meet anybody herself. She raised her eyes cautiously to his. *Was* she in love with him? She'd better not be——

They were in the small breakfast nook off the kitchen. Drew had awakened her and she'd dressed and come out to breakfast, surprised he hadn't already left the homestead. She had been deeply asleep after a long restless night, and a little resentful at being re-called from dreams that were at least more comfortable than reality. Now, looking at the hard implacability of his face, she knew there was no way she could get out of going to the outstation with him, and she got up from the table without saying anything and began to stack up the dishes.

'Leave that,' he said sharply. 'The girls can do it. It doesn't matter about the rest of the house. I want you to get yourself ready right away—we've a long rough drive ahead of us.'

A long rough drive. It needed only that. Edie's head was throbbing, her eyes felt burnt out. Had he even noticed? She doubted it, as she hurriedly tidied her room, straightening the disordered bed that bore witness to the bad night she'd put in. She looked a mess too—and all because of him. It could have been so different this morning, she found herself thinking. But because she was a virgin—because she hadn't given her body to anyone else—he had refused it. Yet shouldn't she be glad? Of course she should be. But she wasn't.

She wanted him badly. She wanted him to—to need her, and somewhere deep within her heart she was convinced that if she became his wife—really his wife —she could make him love her. As she would love him. As she had already begun to love him, in spite of everything.

A tear splashed on the back of her hand and she wiped it away furiously.

She had dressed rather hurriedly when he'd called her, pulling on white jeans and a white T-shirt printed with flowers across the front, and now she wondered if she should change, seeing she was going to be presented to the people at the outstation as Drew's wife. But he'd told her to hurry, so perhaps she wouldn't bother. She looked at herself doubtfully in the glass— a pathetic-looking girl with tear-stained black-shadowed eyes, and not a vestige of sophistication. It was ironic that, because she was the way she was, and hadn't slept around, she had been rejected by her husband. It was even more ironic that she should feel about Drew the way she did, when she had picked him blindfolded.

'You poor little *virgin*,' she told herself pityingly, then swiftly put on her big sunglasses and ran out of the room.

Drew had already driven the station wagon out of the garage, and in less than a minute she was installed beside him and they were on their way.

They had driven some distance in silence when he asked, 'How are you feeling this morning?'

Edie tensed. She was feeling rotten—absolutely rotten—and she was sure she looked it. She told him brightly, 'Fine, thanks. And you?'

'Well, how would you expect?'

'I—I have no idea,' she said, disconcerted.

'Then take note—I'm feeling virtuous,' he said with an ironic quirk to his mouth. 'I can't say I slept well last night, Edie. In fact, I did a lot of thinking.'

'About—what?'

'You, of course. Us.'

Her nerves began to tingle. 'And—and what conclusion did you reach?' she asked with difficulty.

'If you want to know, I reached the conclusion I've been behaving damned badly. I've been pretty rough on you, especially when you consider that the sort of thing I've been doing just wasn't included in the deal we made. It's a conclusion you've possibly reached yourself long ago,' he went on, 'and I can only excuse my behaviour on the grounds that I took certain things about you for granted. The plain fact is, however, that I've done my best to break faith with you.'

He paused and she glanced through the window, and without really taking it in, saw two kangaroos bounding along gracefully by the fence. She realised that what he had taken for granted was that she had slept with other men, but mainly she was pondering the fact that he was apologising for his behaviour. Obviously, he hadn't the least idea how she felt about him.

Dry-lipped, her heart thudding, she stammered out, 'You—you said human emotions were more important than conditions——'

She saw him smile faintly.

'I know I said that. When a man's passion is aroused, he's likely to say almost anything to justify himself,' he said ironically. 'But I suspect you're being sarcastic. I guess you must see me as something of a male chauvinist pig.' She uttered a sound of protest, but he silenced her. 'Oh yes, I'm aware I've ignored your feelings completely—I admit it. I've said it before, but you're not at all the sort of girl I expected to answer an ad like mine.' He was silent as he steered the car deftly through clumps of long spinifex grass—he appeared to have abandoned the wheel tracks they were following, and she thought he must be taking some short cut of his own. 'I really don't quite know what to do with you now,' he resumed presently. 'If you weren't innocent, it would be a great deal simpler,' he concluded almost to himself.

Why? Edie wondered, and the insane idea came into her mind to say, 'I wasn't telling you the truth— I'm not innocent, I'm not a virgin.' She halted on the brink of the lie. Wouldn't he soon find out it wasn't true? Didn't it—hurt the first time if the man wasn't —considerate? And if he thought she'd had a lover before, he wouldn't be all that considerate. He was too passionate; she knew that already. Besides, everything else apart, something in her revolted at telling such a lie—especially, paradoxically, to Drew ...

'I rather think,' he drawled into her troubled thoughts after an interval of several minutes, 'that I'll have to devise some rigid scheme to force me to keep my hands off you. Have you any suggestions, Edie?'

Edie shook her head. She didn't want him to keep his hands off her. What didn't seem to occur to him was that they could agree to make their marriage a marriage for keeps, after all. But perhaps he was sounding her out—giving her an opportunity to make the suggestion herself, if she wanted it that way. Her mind flashed back briefly to the day following their marriage. He had asked her, in the hotel bedroom, if she felt like changing the conditions, and she'd said they suited her perfectly, that she'd made a mistake in coming to Dhoora Dhoora to meet him at all. So now——

She swallowed hard and said with difficulty, 'Couldn't we just—change the conditions, Drew?'

'*What?*'

They were crossing the dry sandy bed of a river and the honey-sweet scent of gum blossoms mingled with the smell of dust as Drew braked suddenly in the shade of the gums and swung round in his seat to give her his full attention. 'Exactly what do you mean, Edie Asher?'

Edie Asher? But wasn't she Edie Sutton? If that was how she had begun to see herself, he evidently saw her differently, and the very fact that he had used her maiden name shook what little confidence she had. She couldn't tell him what she meant, after all. She couldn't propose what she was proposing. Besides, he knew—surely he knew——

His silvery grey eyes narrowed as he moved one hand to lift the concealing sunglasses from her eyes and push them up into her hair. Then he said with a deadly seriousness, 'Do you by any chance mean you're willing to be my wife—for us to sleep together—to procreate?'

Edie thought she'd die of embarrassment. She felt exactly as if she'd been as explicit as he had. Her eyes felt so naked she didn't know what they might tell him if she allowed him to look into them much longer, and in self-defence, she lowered her lashes. She should have kept quiet. She should have forced *him*, subtly, to be the one to suggest they change the conditions, if only so he could make an honest woman of her. The rather ridiculous phrase floated into her mind and for a second she wanted to laugh hysterically. Instead, she tipped the sunglasses back on to her nose and said nothing—and hoped Drew didn't know what an emotional turmoil she was in.

He moved his shoulders, rubbed his chin, and then he said slowly, 'It's a pretty serious decision to make,

Alfreda. After all, we're virtually strangers—even if I have made a couple of very heavy passes at you. Life in the outback is hard in many ways still—I can't deny it. It's certainly not the life you've been used to, and as you said yourself the other day, it's lonely out here. Damnably lonely, sometimes.'

Yes, she had said that, and she couldn't gainsay it. But hadn't his answer been that a woman could be happy having her man come home to her at sundown? She couldn't remind him of that, though. She'd gone far enough already—too far, perhaps, in blatantly offering herself to him when it was true they were strangers. She wished she knew what he was really thinking— then decided it might be as well she didn't.

He was scowling now, his brows drawn down, his eyes narrowed to mere slits as he stared into the glare of the sun beyond their little patch of shade. Her own nerves were quivering by the time he turned back to her to say, 'You're tempting me almost unendurably, Edie, do you know that? It would be just too damned easy to say, We're married, let's get on with it and forget the way it all began. But I think—I really think— we ought to get to know each other better, forget all about being married, admit we're—well, how shall I put it?—mutually attracted to each other physically, and take it from there. Not rush our fences. That way, we might sort ourselves out honourably. It's not going to be easy,' he finished, his eyes going to her lips, 'but if you like, we'll give it a try.'

Edie didn't answer immediately. She found her eyes tangled with his, and it was more the way he was looking at her than the rational-sounding things he was saying that made a wild happiness rise up in her heart. Suddenly, everything looked different. Her headache had gone, the mists were clearing, and she said on a sigh, 'Yes, let's—give it a try.'

Two black and white magpies materialised from the stiff grass on the river bank and flew off together, and she and Drew smiled at each other. Then he started up the motor and drove on.

The sun had grown hot, and soon Edie slept a little as though some problem that had troubled her had been solved.

She didn't wake until, unconsciously registering that the car had come to a halt, she opened her eyes and found someone standing not far from the car window, and a pair of hazel eyes regarding her. It was a girl with short-cut red-gold hair and a boyish figure, a girl who looked to be somewhere in her mid-twenties. A few feet away, Drew stood talking to a man—chunky, bearded, probably younger than he looked. He had laconic blue eyes and a casual yet intelligent air, and he sent Edie a nod and a smile.

Still a little dazed from sleep, she got stiffly from the station wagon, glancing about her as she did so. Tall trees, a gate, a garden—a couple of dogs. A slightly shabby biggish bungalow—the home where Drew had spent his childhood——

Drew moved towards her, took her arm, made the introductions. 'My wife, Edie—Mickie and Damien Shaw.' Smiles, friendliness, a veiled but positive interest in Drew Sutton's bride.

Mickie said cheerfully, 'Come on inside—dinner's just about ready.' She and Edie went ahead into the house. An open door led straight into the living room where an electric fan whirred in the ceiling. There was the faint and tantalising smell of roast beef, and Edie felt pleasantly hungry. She had worried about meeting the people at the outstation, but now she was beginning to feel at her ease. She thought she was going to like the Shaws, and besides, she was happier altogether than she had been when they'd set out this morning.

Mickie showed her to a bathroom—old-fashioned but spotlessly clean—where she could wash up.

'Join the men in the living room when you're ready. Don't worry about me—I've got everything under control in the kitchen.'

This house, Edie thought again, as presently she dried her hands on the guest towel Mickie had provided her with, had once been Drew's home. Drew—— She hadn't yet had time to think back to the new slant his proposition had given to their situation, but now she felt again that small surge of happiness and hope. It wouldn't take them long to get to know each other better, seeing they were so definitely attracted to each other physically—and she was glad he had said that. It was a strange situation. They had to pretend to the Shaws that they were married—and they were going to pretend to each other that they weren't. They were going to forget that. Was it going to be as difficult as Drew imagined? Well, they would soon find that out. Tonight—— Strangely, she felt full of excited anticipation.

After she'd finished in the bathroom she followed her nose to the living room, one end of which served as a dining room. There were just the four of them and dinner was very simple—roast beef and vegetables, queen pudding and cream, and a big pot of tea to follow. Mickie asked about Mrs Wilson and told Drew laughingly that he was lucky he still had someone to have his dinner ready for him when he came home in the evening. Then the men talked about cattle and Edie, even though she knew she should be interested and was, only half listened. Her mind was on other things—on Drew. She enjoyed her dinner, relaxing in the easy atmosphere, and feeling thankful there had been no awkward questions to parry.

When dinner was over, the men got up first. They were going out to some paddock in the jeep, and Drew came to lean over Edie and kiss the back of her neck with a murmured, 'I'll see you later, darling.'

It was the first time he had ever called her darling, and even though she knew the words, and the gesture, were for the benefit of the others, she still felt a thrill run along her nerves. Quick colour came into her face as across the table she caught Mickie looking at her just a little bit speculatively. Well, wouldn't anyone be inclined to speculate about so hasty a marriage? And what, she wondered, if anything, had Drew told them about her? She finished her second cup of tea, then in a kitchen that was not so modern as the one at the main homestead, she helped her hostess with the dishes and they talked a little.

'It's a good set-up at Dhoora Dhoora now,' Mickie remarked presently. 'Are you happy with the new kitchen—and the way Drew's had the inside bathroom updated?' She stopped rather abruptly and turned aside to put some dishes away in the cupboard. Edie had the feeling she was embarrassed and wondered why.

She said lightly, 'Everything's surprisingly modern. I never would have expected to find such comfortable living conditions on a rather remote cattle station. There's not much more one could want, is there?' she finished, reflecting it was as well Mickie didn't know that, whatever the state of the homestead, Drew Sutton's brand new wife just might not have to put up with it for more than a very few weeks.

'Not much,' Mickie agreed with a little smile. She

dried her hands on the kitchen towel. 'Let's go out to the side verandah. We deserve a rest and a cigarette, don't you think?'

Edie agreed that they did. She had begun to feel vaguely uneasy, and she wondered how long the men would be and how she would deal with any personal questions Mickie might ask. After all, she was bound to ask some questions—such as how long she and Drew had known one another and where they had met, she thought nervily.

But Mickie didn't ask any of those embarrassing questions. She remarked, as they both relaxed in comfortable old cane chairs, their sandalled feet resting on the verandah rail, 'It's really great you've come over today. We've been here four years now, and I think Drew's a great guy, so naturally I was dying to know what *you* were like.'

It would have been normal to say something like, 'I hope you approve of me,' but that sort of remark didn't fit this peculiar situation and Edie just couldn't say it. Instead, she said awkwardly, 'I suppose you were— surprised when we got married.'

'Sure we were surprised,' the other girl admitted. 'Drew hadn't said a word—I don't think he'd ever mentioned you. I hope you won't take it the wrong way if I admit I prayed you'd be a bit special—just for his sake.'

Edie coloured deeply. 'I suppose you mean because —because things didn't work out for him before,' she suggested, thinking of Deborah Webster.

Mickie gave her an odd look. 'You do know, then? I wasn't sure, and I wasn't going to mention it, of course——'

'Oh, it's all right—Drew told me,' said Edie, rather surprised, and reflecting a little painfully that Drew must still be carrying a torch for his lost love.

'It's like him to have told you, of course,' Mickie said musingly. 'He's that sort of person, isn't he?—very straight, very honest ... I hope you don't have any guilt feelings about it.'

Guilt feelings? Edie stared at her uncomprehendingly, but Mickie was looking out at the garden and before Edie could say a thing she went on in a very decisive voice, 'In my opinion he and Laurel deliberated far too long before they got engaged.'

Edie almost died of shock. She scarcely heard what Mickie said next—something about Laurel spending two or three months of the year at Dhoora Dhoora.

'What?' she heard herself say vacantly. Somewhere inside her mind everything had gone black. Drew and Laurel had been engaged. She couldn't believe it. When had it happened? And why had he said nothing about it? He hadn't been honest at all—he hadn't been straight, she thought wildly, thinking of that room at the homestead where there were still clothes belonging to Laurel Clarkson—where the scent she used still hung in the air. When had the engagement been broken? It must have been recently—very recently. She felt quite faint as she leaned back in her chair.

'What?' Mickie was echoing, sounding puzzled. 'Oh, you mean about the three months. Well, Laurel's a schoolteacher, so she has these long holidays. Didn't you know?'

'No, I didn't,' Edie said faintly. A million questions were burning holes in her mind—and she couldn't ask any of them, because she'd said Drew had told her about Laurel. How long had they been engaged? When had they broken it off? *Who* had broken it off?

'Drew never gave us a clue everything wasn't going

along smoothly,' Mickie went on, apparently quite unaware of the turmoil in Edie's mind. 'Then one day he
told Dame that Laurel was going to Ireland to visit her
godmother—his aunt Anne, you must know about her
—and that the engagement was off. I was really surprised—I just didn't know who to be sorry for or what
to think when Dame told me. I'm sure I'd have blurted
out questions I had no right to ask if it had been me
Drew told, but you know what men are like. Dame just
listened and minded his own business and said nothing, and of course that's really the best thing to do.
The only thing that bothered both of us was——' She
broke off suddenly and bit her lip, on the point of men-
tioning that rather peculiar will of Philip Sutton's, Edie
realised, and not sure if she would be letting the cat
out of the bag if she did so. Well, that was one thing
Edie knew *all* about ... Mickie finished rather lamely,
'Well, we didn't know about you then, you see.'

'No, I suppose you didn't,' Edie agreed dryly. She
gathered that Mickie must imagine Drew had met her,
fallen in love with her, and broken off his engagement
to Laurel Clarkson, and she wondered what the other
girl would think if she knew the truth. If she asked an
outright question she would have to make up some lie,
she thought distractedly. But to her relief the conversation moved on to safer ground, away from Drew
and Laurel and beginnings, and presently Edie was
talking about nursing and her life in Sydney.

Mickie, it emerged during the next half hour, was a
country girl and had just left school when she met
Damien Shaw at a picnic race meeting on the property
he was managing at the time.

'I was riding in a race where all the jockeys were
girls,' she recalled with evident enjoyment. 'I had a
rather nasty fall and Dame—he's had masses of experi-

ence patching people up in the outback—he came to see if I was dead or only damaged, and that was how we met. Romantic, wasn't it? I'd broken a couple of ribs, actually, and I stayed at the homestead for a week. By that time, neither of us wanted to say goodbye. We got married a month later. That's five years ago now, and we're just about perfectly happy.'

Just about. There was a slightly sad note in her voice as she said that, and Edie wondered if it was because they had no children. Though there was plenty of time for that, surely—Mickie must be only about twenty-four.

A little silence fell and by rights, Edie should be filling it with the story of how she and Drew had met, but she didn't, and presently Mickie said briskly, 'I'm going to make a batch of scones; the men will want something when they come in. I guess you won't be staying late—Drew will want to leave well before dark. It's not a good track to follow at night—too much chance of breaking an axle. I wish I'd suggested you should stay the night, when Dame rang through. That would have been fun, wouldn't it?'

Edie's smile was forced and colour rushed to her face. She and Drew couldn't possibly have stayed the night—they'd be expected to share a room! She said confusedly, 'Oh, we—we couldn't just now. Drew's—he's fairly busy——'

Mickie's eyebrows went up and she said laughingly, 'Come on now, Edie—Drew's the boss, he can delegate the duties. And at *this* time of his life—— Anyhow, he's taken a day off to bring you over here, hasn't he?'

'Not really. I mean, Damien wanted his advice about —about some cattle or something, didn't he?'

'Oh, that was just an excuse, and Drew knows it.' Mickie was still smiling. 'I'd been nagging at Dame because I wanted to meet you, and he kept saying we shouldn't intrude because even if you hadn't gone away, you were on your honeymoon. Then we heard you'd been out at the muster camp, and I said if the men had met you then I was jolly well going to. So Dame gave in ... Anyhow,' she concluded, getting to her feet, 'I'd better get moving and make those scones. You stay here and have a little doze if you feel like it. This heat is trying and you look a bit weary.'

Edie flushed again, but she didn't protest that if she looked weary it wasn't for the reason Mickie probably imagined. All the same, she elected to stay on the verandah rather than go into the kitchen. She had a lot to hide—and as well, she had a lot to think about, and Mickie had no sooner disappeared than her mind returned to the disturbing information she had been given—that until very recently, Drew had been engaged to Laurel Clarkson.

It was strange she should learn it only now, and on the very day when Drew had more or less said they should review the terms of their association. Naïvely, she'd thought there was hope for her. Now she wondered if he were still in love, not with Debbie, but with Laurel. Staring unseeingly across the garden, she visualised the laughing face of the girl in the coloured snapshot—a girl who stood confidently between two men, each of whom had his arm around her. One of whom had loved her enough to ask her to marry him. Drew.

Edie felt a pain in her heart. Who had called the engagement off? Mickie thought it had been Drew—because he'd met and fallen in love with Edie. Edie knew better—and she was certain it must have been Laurel. It suddenly occurred to her that it had been for Laurel that he'd had the bathroom and the kitchen renovated, that the new curtains and soft furnishings in her bedroom had a special significance too.

Her headache was back in full force and she leaned back exhaustedly in her chair and closed her eyes against the afternoon glare. Oh God, it was all so clear now—the reason why he'd put that ad in the paper, the reason why he wasn't interested in a real marriage. It was *his* face he was interested in saving, not Laurel's. And she, Edie—if she'd had any inkling that he was still in love with another girl, a girl who still existed, who wasn't way back in his past like poor dead Deborah, she would never have allowed herself to become so emotionally involved with him, or to respond the way she had to his passionate advances.

And she'd certainly never have proposed to him what she had this morning.

She was unutterably thankful at least that Drew had promised not to take advantage of the fact that they were married. She moved uneasily in the cane chair. They were to get to know each other better before they made any hasty decisions! Well, she thought bitterly, she knew him a whole lot better right now. She knew that he hadn't been honest, he hadn't been fair. He'd only pretended to give her all the facts that night in Narrunga. He'd explained with such apparent frankness why he needed a wife—but he hadn't explained that the reason why he was in such a predicament was because he'd just been jilted. She should have felt sorry for him, but she didn't. She felt betrayed. She felt as shattered as if she had some real claim on him and had discovered he was unfaithful to her.

What a mess it all was! Edie's head ached and she wanted to weep. All her happiness had gone, she didn't trust him any more and she didn't want to get to know him better. When they went home tonight, she'd lock herself up in her room—she'd keep so far away from him it would be nobody's business. He'd get from her exactly what she'd contracted to give, and no more.

CHAPTER SEVEN

WHEN Damien and Drew came back, it was almost dark.

Edie by then was in a quiet turmoil, with Mickie hovering round and murmuring happily that they'd have to stay the night—and making plans for following up the scones with a good filling meal. She interpreted Edie's quiet moodiness as an indication that she was worried something had happened to the men.

'They'll turn up,' the other girl said cheerfully. 'They've probably got so caught up talking cattle and beef they've forgotten the time—and us! I promise you nothing's happened to them. They weren't going all that far and if the car broke down completely—well, they've each got two legs, they're big and strong and all the rest of it. I'm going to make up a bed in one of the spare rooms anyway. Then when they come home we'll all be free to have a good old get-together. I've a really pretty nightie you can borrow, too,' she added cheeringly, 'and there are plenty of toothbrushes in the store, so you won't want for a thing.'

Completely unconvinced, but trying not to show it too much, Edie followed her into the house.

'Don't make up the bed yet, Mickie,' she insisted. 'Really, I'm sure we shan't be staying. Drew's got a lot of things to do——'

Mickie snapped her fingers gaily. 'Oh, Drew can take time off on his honeymoon. Everyone will understand. And at any rate, you just can't drive home in the dark.'

Edie gave up protesting, but when a moment later she heard the sound of a motor, she hurried back to the verandah. Drew would have to see it her way—they couldn't stay here overnight and that was that. Not unless they had separate rooms, and to ask for that was going to take a lot of explaining!

'Well, I don't care,' she thought, 'Drew will have to explain it away somehow.' Or else he would have to say they must leave straight away. That would be easiest.

'What kept you so long?' she heard herself ask sharply as the men came up the steps.

'I guess it's seemed like a thousand years to you, Edie,' said Damien with a good-humoured laugh, and Drew put his arm around her shoulders and tried to pull her against him. She resisted strongly and knew he was both surprised and displeased, but she didn't care.

'Edie's been worried sick,' said Mickie, coming out to join them at that moment. She paused to receive Damien's kiss, then went on lightly, 'I really think she was picturing you both lying dead under the blazing sun, or something like that. What happened to you anyhow? We expected you back ages ago.'

'Oh, we ran into someone who was in a spot of bother,' Drew told her, and Damien put in, 'Bring out a few cans of beer and we'll tell you the whole story. We'll have a wash and a brush up and join you on the verandah in a few minutes. How will that do?'

'But——' Edie began, and then stopped.

'But what?' Drew asked. His grey eyes met hers and she felt a tremor run through her even while she stared back at him. There was something in those eyes she couldn't read. It had always been like that. What was it? The fact that he was still in love with another woman—a living breathing woman, someone he thought about every time he held Edie's body in his arms?

She said weakly, her breath catching, 'Shouldn't we be on our way home, Drew? It's late——'

'It's *too* late, Edie,' Damien put in. 'But don't worry, Edie, Drew and I discussed that on the way home and you're staying the night. Aren't they, Mickie?'

'Of course,' Mickie agreed. By now she was beginning to look distinctly puzzled by Edie's unwillingness to stay the night. 'I'll get that beer.'

They all began to move inside, but Edie put out a hand and caught Drew's arm.

'Drew——'

He turned and looked at her enquiringly, but to her relief the others went on, and she said hurriedly, keeping her voice low, 'Drew, we can't stay the night— you know we can't. Sharing a room, a—a bed——'

He looked down at her quizzically. 'Oh, come on now, Edie, you'd rather we broke an axle—or our necks —driving in the dark. Is that it?'

'No, of course not. But—but surely there's some way that's safe—if you don't take those short cuts——'

'If there's a way then I don't know of it,' he said a little impatiently. 'I'm afraid you'll just have to make the best of it, Edie.'

Make the best of it! Her face went pale, and her nerves suddenly snapped at the prospect of sharing a bedroom with him. 'You mean *you'll* make the best of it,' she accused wildly. 'You arranged this, didn't you? You—you deliberately stayed out till it was too late, in spite of all those promises you made this morning. I'm just beginning to find out I can't trust you one little bit, Drew Sutton!'

'Are you now? And why the devil would that be? What on earth am I supposed to have done this time?' he demanded. He caught hold of her arm with fingers that hurt and stared down angrily into her eyes, and Edie stared back at him, angry too. All sorts of wild accusations concerning his engagement to Laurel floated about in her mind, but before she could get any of them out he grated, 'Damien and I have a valid reason for being back late which you'll hear about presently, no doubt. But while you're accusing me of breaking promises—or intending to break them—I'll remind you that in fact I haven't made you any promises. I'll also remind you—though it's against my principles as a rule to be so ungallantly frank with a member of the female sex—that up to now *I've* been the one who's applied the brake when we were—skidding off the rails. You'd have come to bed with me any time I liked to invite you in the last few days, wouldn't you, Edie? Wouldn't you?'

Oh, how she hated him for reminding her of that! How she hated herself, too, for having fallen so precipitately in love with him. And how certain she was at this exact moment that she could never feel anything for him again other than the deepest dislike.

'Well?' he insisted, and when she refused to answer he pressed on, 'Wasn't it *my* suggestion this morning that we shouldn't rush our fences? Or are you going to tell me it was yours?'

Edie looked at him speechlessly. Her heart was beating suffocatingly fast, and like some little cornered creature she longed to escape. To accuse him now of not being honest with her, of using her to save his face when Laurel had jilted him, seemed futile. He'd have her in a trap in less than no time, and at last she said pantingly, 'I'm—I'm not going to tell you a thing. Except that if you—if you so much as touch me tonight I'll scream the house down!'

He had narrowed his eyes slightly and was looking at her as if she had gone mad.

'What the hell's got into you, Edie?' he asked roughly, shaking her slightly as he spoke. 'I'm damned if I can understand you.'

'I don't care if you can't,' she retorted, pulling away from him. 'I certainly can't understand you, and—and the less we have to do with each other the better. Isn't that about what you said this morning?' she finished bitterly. She scarcely knew what she was saying. Tears had flooded her eyes and she turned her back on him abruptly and looked across the garden. The sun had almost gone, and the light was a fiery red-gold. The whole garden—the lawn, the leaves, the flowers, the trunks of the trees—was glowing and coppery. She breathed deeply and blinked hard to get rid of her tears, and wished despairingly that she'd held herself in check—played it cool. She told Drew chokily, 'You said we'd forget we were married—and that's exactly the way I want it to be.'

'Okay, okay.' His voice still had a hard edge to it. 'So *we* can forget it—but we can't expect Mickie and Dame to do likewise. They think we're happily married lovers and I'm not planning to disillusion them. It doesn't suit me you should do that either, and if you blurt it all out, I'll forget every promise you imagine I ever made to you. Just keep that in mind, will you, Alfreda Asher. We have to share a room tonight and you can shut up and put up with it. It's not a situation that's going to give me much of a kick after all this, I assure you ... And now if you don't mind I'll get washed up. I need that beer.'

She heard him go, though she didn't look at him, and she stood there feeling shaken to the core. He'd never spoken to her this way before, and she hated him for it. And she—she hated Laurel too. Oh, how she hated Laurel Clarkson!

Disgusted with herself, she wanted nothing so much as to go away somewhere alone and have a good cry. Deep down, she wished that they'd never come here—that she'd never heard of Laurel, and more than anything, she dreaded the thought of going to bed that night.

But certainly, she thought, not ten minutes later as they all sat sociably on the verandah, life goes on. On the surface they were two young married couples having a beer together at the end of a hot day. Damien and Mickie could have no suspicion of the dispute she and Drew had engaged in—or of what lay behind it. Sitting back in her chair, willing herself to relax, to calm down, she only half listened to the conversation. She discovered with singularly little interest that Drew and Damien certainly had a good reason for being late back home. They'd been out to the muster camp and it was on the way back, taking a different track because Drew wanted to look at a certain bore, that they'd been delayed.

'We ran into this young bloke in a beat-up old car who'd got himself stranded,' Damien explained. 'Apparently he'd been there since morning and it took us God knows how long to fix up his vehicle and put him on his way again.' He went on to enlarge upon the difficulties they'd had and Edie ceased to listen. Drew, sitting back drinking his beer, left the story to Damien, and Edie wondered if he was thinking about her—hating her as she was hating him—or if his mind was on what the other man was saying. Hers certainly wasn't. It was going round and round in circles as she tried to make sense of her mixed emotions and failed dismally. She was sure she hated Drew—she had to hate him; he'd behaved abominably——

Her eyes strayed to him continually, lingering on that smoky brown hair, his tanned face, the strong lean line of his jaw, the dark hair that showed on his chest where he had unbuttoned his shirt for coolness. He was like no other man who had ever been in her life, and in a frighteningly short space of time she had become so—so fanatically addicted to him that this feeling of hating him was almost as exciting as her previous feeling of loving him—of wanting him. Now she wanted to fight him, and her mind went back over their low-pitched conversation on the verandah so short a time ago. She remembered every expression that had passed over his face, every note that had come into his voice—the feel of his fingers on her arm, the threat that if she poured it all out she'd regret it. A shudder ran through her and her thoughts jetted ahead to the time when they'd be shut in alone in the bedroom . . .

With a start, she realised she must have been wrapped up in her thoughts for a considerable time. The story of the stranded traveller was long over, the beer cans were empty, and Mickie was promising that the meal would be on the table in five minutes flat.

The remainder of the evening passed in a kind of dream. Edie's preoccupation was taken to mean she was tired, and she wasn't teased over her lack of response when Mickie or Damien tried to draw her into the conversation. She wondered what they'd say to each other later—whether Mickie would perhaps decide Drew had made a mistake in breaking with Laurel to settle for her. Laurel, who'd stayed at Dhoora Dhoora so often, would never have been such an outsider. Was she—was she good in bed? The question came into her mind as clearly as if someone had spoken it, and she looked up in alarm and coloured fiercely as she met Drew's eyes—cool and unreadable. She pretended to yawn, covering her mouth with her hand, and Mickie said sympathetically, 'We're keeping you up too late. You must have made an early start this morning.'

'Yes, I am tired,' Edie admitted. 'I wonder if you'd excuse me if I went to bed now.'

'Of course,' Mickie agreed. 'It's time we were all hitting the hay anyhow. When we have visitors we tend to forget the time and stay up talking till all hours. Does anyone feel like a nightcap?'

Nobody did, it seemed, and instead of being able to say goodnight, and to escape, Edie found herself making her way to the bedroom Mickie had prepared in Drew's company. If he'd been considerate, she thought, he'd have told her to go ahead while he took a walk in the garden, or something like that. But he didn't, and she supposed he wanted to give the impression he was eager to be alone with his bride. He had taken her arm, but she soon pulled away from him and told him aloofly, 'You don't have to come to bed yet just because I'm tired.'

He didn't bother to answer her but pushed open the door, and as she went in ahead of him he flicked on the switch that lit a wall lamp over the dressing table. Then he shut the door and leaned against it and looked at her with a cold clinical expression in his eyes that was totally alien to her. She almost withered under it and for a minute she didn't move. Suddenly the night seemed deadly quiet. Mickie's and Damien's room, she knew, was at the other end of the passage and all she could hear was her own breathing.

Then there came the far-off but familiar call of a mopoke, and as if a spell had been broken she moved across the room. On the bed, which was covered by a heavy old-fashioned white crocheted bedspread, was a pretty blue nightgown, and Edie averted her eyes from it quickly. Scarcely knowing what she was doing, she leaned down and pressed her hands against the mattress, as though testing it for comfort.

'Do you want me to sleep on the floor again?' Drew asked in a voice so cold it sent splinters of ice into her heart.

She straightened up and told him, 'If you don't, then I shall.'

'That leaves me no choice, does it?' He strode across the room, pulled back the bedspread and tossed one of the pillows on to the floor. 'I want to take a shower before I turn in. You go first if you want to—I promise I shan't intrude.'

She said nothing and he added, his voice and his eyes hard, 'But I forgot—my promises mean nothing, do they?'

Edie swallowed and looked away. The amosphere between them, that had often been tense and had gone through many stages since they had met, had never been as disastrous as this, and she found herself longing to have even last night's situation back again. Last night she had felt so wounded, so frustrated, because he had let her go to bed alone! Could it have been only last night? It didn't seem possible. It was her own fault, of course, for stirring things up as she had this evening —and she'd done that because she was stunned by what she'd learned from Mickie. The fact was, she had become far too emotional about it, and now she made things worse than ever by saying quarrelsomely, 'You're always saying you never make promises. Anyhow, there's sure to be a lock on the bathroom door and I'll certainly use it.'

'I'd advise you to since you don't trust me,' he said coldly.

Edie's cheeks went crimson and then white. She picked up the shamefully sexy nightgown, and promised herself she'd wear bra and panties under it, seeing she had no slip with her. Then she gathered up the toilet things left for her by the thoughtful Mickie, and catching sight of a towelling bathrobe hanging behind the door she took that too. She slung out of the room and only just managed to restrain herself from slamming the door shut.

Her legs shook as she made her way to the bathroom, which she found unoccupied. There was a bolt on the door and she used it, just in case—because you never knew with Drew, she told herself.

She took her time over her shower, letting the warm water run soothingly over her body and planning that she'd be in bed and asleep—or pretending to be asleep —when Drew came back from the shower. She tried not to think of him sleeping on the floor—and she tried not to think of him sleeping in the bed. There'd been no pyjamas laid out for him. He'd wear his briefs, she supposed, and banished the vision of his muscular figure that floated into her mind.

As she dried herself on the big bathtowel, she knew that some way her heart was sore. It shouldn't have been like this tonight—oh, it shouldn't! Only this morning she'd been so happy because of what Drew had suggested. It would have been so different sharing a room if there'd been an understanding between them.

He might have made love to her, she admitted to herself with a feeling of shame—and then reminded herself she should be thankful she'd found out about his duplicity in time.

Ask him about Laurel, a voice within her advised. He owes it to you to tell you. Yet did he? Did he owe anything to a girl who had merely answered an ad?

There was some scented talc on the vanity cabinet and she used it absentmindedly before she slipped the nightgown on, rejecting her previous impulse to wear panties and bra under it. It wasn't necessary—Drew wasn't going to see her. She wouldn't discard the bathrobe till he was out of the way.

A minute later she made her way back to the bedroom. Before she went in she tapped on the door. There was no answer and she went in. The room was empty, and she stared about her disbelievingly. It was somehow an anticlimax. The bedspread had been folded up and now lay on top of the chest. A corner of the sheet and the single light blanket was turned back, the wall lamp was off, but on one of the bedside tables a reading lamp shed a soft glow over the room. Where had he gone? To walk in the garden and give her the privacy she wanted to shed her bathrobe and slip into bed?

Curiously, she felt uneasy. She'd sooner have found him there—brushed her hair at the mirror, perhaps asked him in some indirect way about Laurel while he collected his things for the shower. That would be the way to do it—indirectly. She didn't want to put Mickie in for being indiscreet—because she hadn't been indiscreet.

She dropped her clothes on a chair with uncharacteristic carelessness, then went to the verandah door and looked out.

'Edie.'

His voice made her jump. He was standing some feet away in deep shadow where the vines shrouded the verandah so thickly she hadn't noticed him.

'What?' Her voice shook oddly, and she felt a tingling sensation in her limbs.

'Come here. I want to talk to you.'

She stayed where she was. 'Why don't you come here?'

He leaned back against the rail and she could see his face vaguely, and the white flash of his teeth more distinctly.

'You really want to know why not?' He moved towards her as he spoke and stopped where the soft light from the bedroom fell on him, and she caught her breath. He had stripped off his shirt and the sight of his bare chest was somehow unnerving.

'Yes—why?' she said unevenly, though by now she hardly knew what she was talking about.

'Because there's a bed in there, that's why, Edie. That's one thing that's generally been missing on the other occasions I've started making love to you.'

She flinched a little. 'You're—you're not going to——'

'Make love to you tonight?' he finished for her. 'I'd hardly want to when you've been acting like a she-devil ever since I came in this evening. No, I'm not in the mood for making love to you right now, Edie, but that's not to say I won't feel that way later on.'

'You—you were going to take a shower,' she said, feeling nervous perspiration break out on her palms. It was impossible in the midst of a conversation like this to frame some seemingly casual question about his recent love life. She simply couldn't do it.

'It can wait. Maybe I'm going to need a shower later on—a cold one,' he said with a brutal realism. 'Meanwhile, are you going to join me out here, or are you going to insist we go into the bedroom?'

'What—what do you want?'

'To talk to you, that's all.'

'What about?' she asked suspiciously.

'When you come over here you'll discover what about.'

She shivered. 'I—I don't know that I want to discover it. I'm ready for bed.'

'Well, damn you, Edie, I'm not!' he exclaimed with shocking suddenness. 'My share of it's a pillow on the floor.'

Her mouth opened soundlessly and then she was free to choose no longer, for he had taken her forcibly by the arm and pulled her violently away from the doorway. 'You can come and talk to me and quit playing whatever crazy game it is you've begun.'

'I don't know what you're talking about,' she gasped, as whether she liked it or not she was dragged across the verandah.

'We should be out of earshot here,' he said when he'd drawn her round the corner. 'Now we can start talking, and the first thing I want to know is what the hell got into you tonight?'

He still kept hold of her arm and she stared into the darkness of his eyes, feeling her breast palpitating.

'What—what do you mean?' she breathed.

'You know damned well what I mean—all those accusations you hurled at me, suggestions of foul intentions and broken promises, of not being able to trust me. What's it all about? I've admitted to behaving badly, but I haven't seduced you, have I? Not yet,' he added beneath his breath, for without apparently meaning to, he had taken her other arm and pulled her against him. 'You can't have forgotten you all but asked me to do more or less that only this morning.'

'I—I did no such thing,' she panted.

'Edie, don't tell such lies. You were still stirred up enough after last night to suggest we—consummate our marriage.'

She flinched. 'I didn't mean that.'

'Oh yes, you did. That's exactly what you meant and we both know it. Yet when I came in this evening you started hurling abuse at me—threatening what you'd do if I so much as touched you tonight. Well, I'm touching you now, aren't I?' he asked, his voice rough. He pulled her even closer and his eyes seemed to pin her like a butterfly. 'Are you going to scream the house down?' He said no more as his lips found hers, and for a moment the two of them wrestled together. Edie twisted and turned her head in vain. His lips followed hers and captured them, and then his hands were inside her robe seeking her breasts. His fingers stroked down over her rib cage to the softness of her belly, and she stopped resisting. It was completely mad, but her mind seemed to have cut out. All that was left was her body and the sensations he was arousing in it.

'You said,' she gasped out as he left her mouth free for a moment simply because he needed to draw breath, 'you said you wouldn't make love to me tonight——'

'I won't—if you don't want me to.' His voice was muffled and his breath against her bare shoulder made her realise that somehow her bathrobe had slipped to the floor. 'Anyhow, I never make love to a woman with a verandah rail against my back.'

'What woman? Laurel?' The crazy words came into her mind, but she didn't speak them, though the recollection of Laurel was enough to bring her at least partially to her senses. She withdrew her hands from where, she discovered, they were rhythmically stroking the muscled bareness of his back, and began to push at his chest, feeling his skin firm and exciting under her hands. 'Let me go—you said we had to talk.'

To her shocked surprise, he raised his head almost instantly.

'Oh God! Why do you do this to me, Edie?'

'Do what?' She almost sobbed it out. 'You're—it's you—— You—you never mean what you say——'

'You're my wife,' he groaned. 'I've tried to forget it, but I can't.'

'I'm not your wife—I took your name to do you a favour——'

'Edie.' He put his hands ungently on either side of her face and looked at her penetratingly through the darkness. She could feel his eyes probing into hers—into her very soul. 'Legally you're my wife. That's basic and I can't get past it. Five minutes ago I was angry—cold. Now you're in my arms and I want you—and you want me. Will you come to bed with me?'

Something inside her ached and ached. She longed to say yes, to lean her head against the nakedness of his chest, to have him lift her in his arms and carry her to the bedroom and make the most violent love to her. It was all she wanted in this life. Yet she loathed the idea of having him use her body if his heart belonged to someone else.

'No,' she said. '*No*. Don't touch me!'

And then she hurt all through when his hands fell from her and he said with a contempt that ate into her heart like acid, 'The way you say that! When only this morning you as good as said you didn't want me to keep my hands off you. What's happened in the meantime?'

'*Nothing*,' she insisted. 'You were wrong, that's all. I don't want you to touch me—not ever again.'

Yet she did, she did—she wanted it more than anything. But how could she want it? She was nothing to him—even now he might be thinking about Laurel, remembering the feel of her body against his. Oh yes, Edie had read enough to know that men—and women —pretended they were in some other lover's arms even when they were carried away on a tide of passion.

But she wasn't going to have Drew Sutton ride out his passion on her with Laurel Clarkson in his mind.

She put her head up and reminded him unsteadily, 'You said we'd forget we were married.'

'And I said it wouldn't be easy—and now I know it's damned well impossible,' he said between his teeth. 'But okay, little virgin—I don't pretend to know what this is all about, but we'll play it your way. Run along —you can have that big bed all to yourself. You can curl up all by yourself and go to sleep. You will, I suppose,' he added scorchingly, 'without the slightest trouble.'

He stooped and picked up the bathrobe and flung it unceremoniously across her shoulders. 'Cover yourself up, for God's sake!'

Edie clutched the garment to her, her breath uneven, and all but ran back to the bedroom. She was in bed with clothes pulled up to her chin by the time Drew reached the doorway, and despite herself she stared back at him as he stood looking across at her.

'I suppose you have no idea what kind of a picture you make,' he said savagely, 'lying there with your dark hair spread out on the pillow and those beautiful eyes so wide and frightened. Do you think I'm such a brute I'm determined to—have my way with you, regardless of your wishes?'

Edie didn't answer. She could feel her heart beating violently against her ribs and she was positive he must be able to see its movement under the light bedclothes. His chest gleamed darkly and his eyes glittered as though enchanting her, and she stared and stared at him, feeling faintly dizzy. The clamouring bells of her senses made her aware of an almost maddening desire to accept those broad shoulders, those narrow hips. She wanted his mouth on hers, his hands discovering her body—hers discovering his. Suppose he *had* deceived her? Suppose he *was* ready to make believe she was Laurel—why should she care, so long as they could lie together in the darkness discovering delight——

Oh God! With a stifled groan she turned on her side away from the sight of him. She was sick—really sick —to keep thinking this way, as if she had no pride, no dignity—as if the gratification of the senses was all that mattered.

She heard him move further into the room, saw his shadow on the wall as he picked up soap and towel, heard the soft click of the door as he closed it behind him.

She lay as she was, on her side, half curled up, agonising. What would it be like to be properly married to him, instead of having to go through this subtle form of torture? Why didn't he just make love to her, if that was what he wanted? But he would, of course. She had only to say yes.

But she'd said no, and he'd accepted it. Or had he? Was it as simple as all that? Was he going to leave her alone tonight? She knew enough about him already to be aware his passion was easily aroused.

It seemed a lifetime before he came back from the shower.

'Are you asleep, Edie?'

She shook her head, not turning to look at him, though her heart leapt a little. He wasn't going to leave her alone, and she was ready to turn to him when he said levelly, 'To set your mind at ease, we'll go home tomorrow. You'll have your own room there, and I shall be able to sleep in a bed.'

He switched out the light and she lay quivering, frustrated. He was going to lie down on the floor and she couldn't bear it. She was quite sure she had only to say, 'Don't sleep there—come into the bed', and he'd come. But of course she wasn't going to say any such thing. It would be worse—far worse—than what she'd said this morning.

All the same, half a minute later, she said it.

'Drew, don't sleep on the floor—please———'

His reply was a half smothered exclamation that made her recoil.

'For God's sake, I've had enough trauma for tonight! You've made your choice and I've accepted it. Just don't push your luck too far. Go to sleep and shut up.'

She didn't reply. She felt utterly humiliated.

Of course she couldn't go to sleep. Long, long after she could hear from his quiet even breathing that he was asleep, she lay restless in the big bed. She thought endlessly of Drew—and of Laurel. Perhaps they'd ended their engagement by mutual agreement—perhaps he'd really meant it when he'd said this morning they should get to know each other better before they took the serious step of making their marriage a real one. Yet how could she believe him when less than twenty-four hours later he was asking her to come to bed with him?

When finally she slept it was through sheer exhaustion.

CHAPTER EIGHT

SHE slept in late in the morning, and Mickie finally came in with breakfast on a tray and woke her. Drew's pillow was on the bed beside hers, and a quick almost guilty look around assured Edie there was no sign he had spent the night on the floor. He had very evidently made sure of not giving himself away!

'Did you sleep well?' Mickie asked, and Edie said she had, and hoped she didn't look as haggard as she felt.

'The men went out a couple of hours ago,' Mickie told her. 'Drew said you were so sound asleep he didn't wake you. They should be back any time now. It's a pity he wants to get back to Dhoora Dhoora so soon. I'd have loved to have you stay another day, but I guess there'll be other times.'

'Yes, of course,' Edie agreed automatically. She was relieved to know Drew wasn't about, that she wouldn't have to face him just yet, and give the appearance of being a happy bride. Much as she liked Mickie, she hoped they'd leave for home the minute Drew came in.

Mickie offered to lend her some clean clothes, but she refused with a show of gratefulness. 'There's no point really—we'll be home today, so I can make out.'

'Well, I'll leave you to dress,' the other girl said. 'Have you had enough to eat? I'm afraid I took it for granted you weren't a big breakfast eater.'

'Oh, I'm not—I've had plenty,' Edie assured her, having found she had to force herself to eat even the toast and marmalade Mickie had brought her.

Once she was alone, she climbed out of bed and looked at herself rather anxiously in the mirror. She hadn't slept well, and no amount of trying could persuade her she looked like a happy bride who had spent the night in her husband's arms. Her face was pale and there were shadows under her dark eyes. Heaven knew how Mickie had interpreted her decidedly fragile air.

More to keep herself out of the way if Drew should come back than for any other reason, she took a shower and got back into her white jeans and T-shirt. She combed her hair and put on some lipstick, but as she hadn't brought her eye make-up with her there was nothing she could do to disguise those shadows. She was still at the mirror when she heard the sound of a motor, and the blood rushed to her face and then subsided. She felt she couldn't go out to meet Drew, not even for the sake of appearances. She would just have to make some excuse when she finally had to appear.

She folded the bedclothes slowly, and put the quilt back on the bed and was wondering what she could do next when Mickie came to the door.

'How's it going, Edie? The men are having a beer. Drew sent me to tell you to get a move on—he's just about ready to go.'

Edie gave her a bright smile. 'I'm sorry if I've kept anyone waiting. I was just tidying up a little.'

'That's sweet of you,' said Mickie. 'But you shouldn't have bothered.'

Drew got to his feet and came over to greet her like a loving husband as she came on to the verandah with Mickie. Nervously she watched him stride across to her, his silver-grey eyes examining her face so minutely and so intimately she wanted to disappear through the floor. All that had happened between them last night seemed to unfold in her mind like the re-running of a film, and her feelings were in complete confusion as he put his arms around her and lowered his face to kiss her. He hadn't shaved, and the roughness of his jaw rasped against her soft skin and she felt a shiver go through her and wished in sudden despair that she was safely asleep again.

Only a few minutes later they had said goodbye and were on their way home, and in no time Edie became aware of the distance that existed between them. He had kissed her in front of the others, but now the coolness of his attitude was showing and it made her shrivel up inside.

'I hope you've enjoyed your taste of female company,' Drew said almost heavily after a silence that had lasted a long time. It had been getting on Edie's nerves, and yet she had found herself unable to break it, even though she was uneasily aware that he probably felt she owed him some explanation for her behaviour.

'Yes, I—I like Mickie,' she said with an effort at naturalness. 'She told me she and Damien have been here four years. I suppose you must all know each other pretty well.'

'Pretty well,' he agreed, his tone polite but still distinctly distant to her sensitive ears. 'Dame's a man I can trust implicitly, and I've a lot of time for Mickie. She's the sort of girl who gets on with almost anyone. There's no worse disaster in the outback than a woman who's a mischief-maker, and there isn't a malicious bone in her body.'

Edie digested this. He was right about Mickie. She was sweet—sweet and tactful, and it wasn't her fault she had told Edie something that Drew, evidently, hadn't intended she should know. She knew it would be very mean of her now to mention Laurel Clarkson in any way that could make him suspect Mickie had been telling tales. Frowningly, she stared out at the pink and straw-coloured grasses woven together over the soft red of the earth. The golden gleam of wattle blossom and the flame of new gum tips against the sun caught her eye as he said laconically, 'I'd cast you among the non-mischief-making group too, as a matter of fact.'

Edie felt herself start. That was a compliment, and somehow she hadn't expected him to have anything nice to say about her this morning.

'Would you?' she asked, and then added without really meaning to, 'I suppose you mean you trusted me not to tell Mickie about—about us. How we met, I mean,' she corrected herself hastily.

'I guess that's right,' he agreed. He didn't ask if she had told Mickie, so she didn't tell him. Instead she remarked with an oblique look at his profile, 'It must be nice to feel you can trust people like that.'

He turned his head and caught her eye. 'I get the feeling you're telling me—and not very subtly either— that *you* don't trust me.'

She was telling him that—but her mistrust lay in a different direction from the obvious one.

'I'd like to know why,' he said reasonably. 'You seemed happy enough after we'd talked in the car yesterday. Now you appear to be having second thoughts. Is it too much to ask to know the reason?'

It was too much. She could hardly say, Mickie told me about you and Laurel Clarkson, so she said aloofly, 'I don't have to explain myself to you. It's not as if we were——'

'Married? Engaged?' he suggested mockingly when she stopped. 'All the same, you're not being very co-operative, are you? It does help a relationship if people are honest with each other.'

Honest! Edie thought cynically, and she almost laughed. He could talk about being honest! She said, 'We don't have a relationship,' and she saw his eyebrows go up.

'For God's sake, who do you think you're fooling? We have a relationship all right. Which reminds me— just don't invite me to share your bed again while you're feeling this way, will you? Next time, I might take you up on it—and spoil our relationship completely,' he finished grimly.

After that they didn't talk at all. Edie sat dumbly beside him wanting to cry and wishing she had never heard of Laurel Clarkson. It had poisoned everything —just at the moment when they had been getting on to a steadier footing. Now there was an unbearable tension between them. She thought of the peace of the flat back in Sydney—of Barb, of the patients she had nursed, of her quiet orderly life, and she felt a longing to be back there. She even thought of Joe and of how uncomplicated he was. But deep in her heart she knew it would be impossible to go back now. She would stay on here until the game was played out one way or another—till she won Drew or lost him. Though at the moment it looked very much as if she had lost him already.

Drew went out that afternoon without telling her he was going, or even saying goodbye to her. She only knew he had gone because she heard the car. Well, he could come and go as he pleased, she wasn't really his wife, as she had pointed out to him more than once. All the same she felt foolishly hurt, and when she had washed the lunch dishes, she spent the rest of the afternoon sitting listlessly in the shade in the garden. She thought constantly about Drew and Laurel and with difficulty resisted an impulse to go into that bedroom again. Once there, she would only torment herself with further thoughts of the two of them together. Instead she tried to think out why on earth Laurel had left him. It was incomprehensible.

He was back home earlier than she expected him, and he came straight out to the garden in search of her. He stopped within a few feet of where she sat and she looked up, her heart beating fast, to find him smiling at her distantly.

'I collected the mail from the box on my way home, Edie,' he said briskly instead of greeting her. 'I'll be sorting it out in the office, so if you like to come along presently you can collect anything that's arrived for you.'

'Thank you,' she said stiffly, almost hating him for his politeness.

'Did you have a restful afternoon?' he asked, his eyes expressionless.

'Yes, thank you,' she said again, and hoped her bitterness didn't show on her face.

He went, and she waited almost half an hour before she went inside. She hoped a little wistfully that there would be a letter from Barb, but she didn't expect to hear from anyone else, as no one knew where she was. The office door was open and Drew sat at his desk, absorbed in a letter he was reading. He had sorted the mail into various piles and she was amazed to see how much of it there was. There were parcels and packets as well as letters, and as she waited for him to acknowledge her presence, she pondered on them, and decided they must be for all the stockmen and various people who worked on the station. Drew would have to take the mail out to the muster camp—or down to the stock-men's bungalows.

She moved slightly and he looked up, his grey eyes abstracted.

'Oh, you're there. Only one letter for you, Edie,' he said, and handed it to her absentmindedly.

'Thank you,' she said automatically. She hesitated a moment, but he had returned to his own correspon-dence, and rather frustratedly she went back through the house to the side verandah and stood there to read her letter. It was from Barb, of course, but as she read it only half her mind was on it. The other half was back in the office with Drew, and she was picturing that faraway look in his eyes and wondering who his letter had been from. She knew so little about him—it was almost nothing. She knew the names of only a few people in his life—his aunt Anne, his cousin Greg—Laurel——

She blinked away her fancies and forced her atten-tion back to her own letter, but had to start reading it again. Barb had received her note from Narrunga but was plainly concerned about what was going on. 'Honestly, Edie,' she read, 'you shouldn't play on my nerves this way. One little note that tells me exactly nothing. What's happening? I'm getting worried—I mean it. I feel guilty about having let you do such an idiotic thing. What kind of guy is this cattleman if he's not what we expected? For heaven's sake, *let me know*. And if he's not rushing you to the altar, as you said, then what's going on? *Please write*.

'You might be interested to know that Joe's been to the flat several times. He wants to know where you are and he's threatening all sorts of things if I don't tell him soon. He's a nice bloke, Edie—I think he really does want to marry you. I wish you'd come back, and

though what you decide is up to you, of course, it
seems to me it's the most sensible thing to do.' The remainder of the letter was chit-chat about the hospital
and various mutual acquaintances, and Edie skimmed
through it rather quickly. The old life seemed very
far away and very unreal, and the fact that Joe was apparently having second thoughts about marriage didn't
interest her at all. But she was sorry Barb was so worried—she had repeated that in a postscript—and she
promised herself she'd write to her that night. What
exactly she'd tell her, she had no idea. The truth wasn't
going to be very reassuring, that was certain!

But what was the truth? That she was married—to
a stranger—and that she'd be unmarried again very
shortly. Oh God, what a secret to have on your conscience if ever you wanted to marry again! How would
Joe feel about her, for instance, if he knew of this—
adventure? Well, she'd never be interested in marrying
him—or anyone else, come to that, she told herself
despairingly ...

Over dinner, Drew was as polite as he had been
when he had spoken to her earlier, and he was still
abstracted. Some way or other, he managed to keep the
conversation impersonal and to avoid awkward silences.
No one listening to them, Edie thought, would ever
dream they were married, had felt passion for each
other, had groaned against each other's lips. If Drew
was getting back to his idea that they should forget
their marriage, then he was doing so with a vengeance.
But he had plainly abandoned the idea that they should
aim for a better understanding of each other.

Afterwards, he complimented her conventionally
on the meal she had cooked, but he didn't offer to help
with the washing up, which, instead of leaving it to the
girls, she decided to do herself. She wasn't sure if he

expected her to join him in the sitting room afterwards, and she was very much tempted to go to her room. Except that if she did so, he might follow her there to see what the trouble was. And even in his present mood, she didn't want him in her bedroom. She didn't trust him, and still less did she trust herself.

She finally found a writing pad, took her letter from Barb, and went determinedly into the sitting room.

He was there—leaning back in a chair, a glass in his hand, the whisky decanter and a small jug of water on the low table beside him. He wore black pants and a violet silk shirt, and he looked absolutely stunning. Edie couldn't keep her eyes off him—that tanned skin, that thick wave of smoke-brown hair. He was somehow more masculine than any man she had ever known, which was weird in a way, with that pretty violet shirt. He had worn a black tie at dinner, but he had discarded it and the three top buttons of his shirt were undone revealing the thick hair on his chest.

He didn't look up as she came in, but stared moodily at the glass in his hand, and she studied him for a long moment, aware of the quickening beat of her heart. He was her husband, she found herself thinking. They were legally married. Why should she worry about his past—about Laurel Clarkson? Couldn't she apologise, start again, persuade him to——

She pulled up her thoughts quickly. What she wanted and what he wanted could very easily be two different things.

After a few seconds, she went to sit on the couch near the reading light, settling her writing pad on her lap and smoothing down her long skirt over her knees, admiring for a moment its lovely burnt orange colour.

He lifted his head and smiled at her slightly, raising one eyebrow in a way that had become familiar to her.

'Washing up finished?' he asked.

She nodded. 'I'm going to write a letter,'

'Who to?' He narrowed his eyes and leaned forward to pour himself another whisky.

'To my flatmate. My—my letter was from her.'

'I guessed as much. The writing looked like a woman's ... Would you like a drink?'

'No, thank you.'

He didn't push it, but asked abruptly, shifting his position so he was looking straight at her, 'What did your flatmate have to say?'

Edie blinked. 'Nothing much.'

'Oh, come on—she must have had something to say. Didn't you write to her from Narrunga—before we were married?'

'Yes.'

'Well then——'

Edie stared back at him frustrated. What right had he to question her about her personal letters? None, as far as she could see. No more right than she had to question him about his. But as he continued to hold her gaze, she said unwillingly, 'She wants to know what's happening, that's all.'

'I suppose she does. She knows all about your answering my advertisement, doesn't she? I remember you said it was she who had pointed it out to you.' He took a gulp of his whisky and looked at her fixedly over the glass. 'And what's happening in Sydney? Any news of the boy-friend you were consigning to limbo?'

'Yes,' she said after a moment. She wet her lips. 'As a matter of fact, he's—he's changed his ideas about marriage.'

The expression in his eyes altered slightly.

'You mean he wants to marry you now?'

'I—I suppose so.'

'Then that's too bad for him—because you're married already. Does he know that?'

'No,' she said unwillingly. She wished he wouldn't continue to look at her that way. Her nerves were screaming and she couldn't concentrate on what she was saying. After a silence that seemed to have become dangerous, she asked him wildly, 'Who was your mail from? Or—or do you object to my asking?'

'Not at all,' he said, his eyes still darkly on hers. 'My mail's mostly business, in any case.'

'Mostly?' she repeated, thinking of the letter he had been reading so absorbedly in the office.

'Yes, mostly. But if you're curious——'

'No more curious than you are,' she interrupted, defensively.

'—then the only personal mail I had was from Ireland. My dear aunt sees fit now and again to let me know what's happening over there on the other side of the world,' he concluded, a sardonic twist to his mouth.

'Have you—let her know you're married?' she asked jerkily, remembering that Laurel was in Ireland too.

'No, I have not,' he said shortly, and returned his attention to his whisky glass,

So he hadn't told his aunt. So Laurel didn't know. What did it all mean? she wondered. But of course, this marriage was merely a stratagem to attain a certain end—it wasn't the sort of marriage you wanted to broadcast. All the same, his aunt was concerned, since her son would inherit Dhoora Dhoora if Drew didn't. Well, it was his business, and plainly he wasn't going to talk to her about it. She opened her writing pad determinedly.

'Dear Barb,' she wrote, 'I'm sorry I didn't write sooner, but as you might guess the mail doesn't go out from here very often.' She paused. What came after that? How could she explain the situation to Barb in terms that made it sound reasonable, even acceptable? Or would she skate over the whole thing and not tell her anything? But Barb was a good friend and she was genuinely worried, and she deserved better than evasions that were no more than lies.

After a little thought, she continued slowly, 'It was lovely hearing all the news from you. (Like hearing news from another planet, her thoughts told her.) It's funny about Joe, isn't it? It just shows you. About Drew Sutton—my cattleman——' She paused again. My cattleman. She didn't dare raise her eyes to look at him, but she was aware he had tossed down his whisky and poured himself another one, and she had the distinct and uneasy feeling he was watching her.

'We're married,' she wrote recklessly. 'I expect you'll think I'm out of my mind, but the fact is he had to get married for a specific reason that's to do with this property. I won't bore you with all the details now, but it was rather urgent and as I'd answered the ad and he'd sent the tickets, it really wouldn't have been fair to back out. I know you'll find it hard to understand, and I can't really explain how I fell for it, but he's not just any old cattleman. He's terribly good-looking and attractive, in fact. But don't worry—I'll try not to lose my head. It's only a temporary thing—the marriage will be annulled in a few weeks. I'm not gullible enough to think he wants to make it permanent. Don't give Joe my address—I'll be back.'

She raised her lashes cautiously to look across at him, and with a shock that went right through her she encountered his eyes and saw in them a look so hotly and openly sexy she couldn't help knowing what he was thinking about.

She blushed, slowly and deeply, to the very roots of

her hair, yet she didn't look away. She didn't want to. She could feel all the primitive urges within her surfacing, and her awareness shifted from outside to the most sensitive nerve ends of her system. It was shocking, so suddenly and without warning, to want him like this—to long for him to come and take her in his arms and make love to her. To be unable to deny it even to herself because her body wouldn't allow any denials.

She should have stayed in her room. She knew it now. She shouldn't have come to join him here, where he could sit and drink his whisky and stare at her—and she could raise her eyes and stare at him . . .

When he moved eventually it was not to get up and come to her. He merely put down his empty glass and leaned towards her, his legs apart, his forearms on his thighs, his hands lightly clasped.

'Who's the letter for? Your flatmate? Or—Joe?' he asked a little thickly.

'My—my flatmate,' she said, her voice sounding unnatural in her own ears.

'What are you telling her?'

'About us,' she said, reluctantly.

'Show me.' He shifted his position and reached out his hand.

Instantly she drew back her hands covering the sheet of notepaper. 'No! It's none of your business.'

'But it is,' he insisted unsmilingly. 'You're writing about us. Come on—I want to see what you've said.'

She shook her head, but he stood up and now he was looking down at her with purpose in his eyes, and she suspected he was at least a little drunk.

'I want to know what's going on in your mind.' he said. 'You won't tell me—perhaps your letter will.'

'It won't tell you a thing you don't know,' Edie said quietly, but he reached down for her wrist and pulled her mercilessly to her feet, his free hand grabbing for the writing pad that she'd automatically put behind her back.

There was a brief struggle. She heard herself utter a sob as the writing pad fell to the floor and her body was locked with his. She twisted her head aside, aware of the smell of whisky as the warmth of his breath touched her brow, then abruptly her resistance went. She lowered her head with a soft moan and leaned her cheek against his chest, feeling the roughness of the hair inside the opening of his shirt. Her eyes were closed and she could feel the blood pounding at her temples, pounding through her veins. She heard the beat of his heart and felt the rise and fall of his chest under her cheek as their bodies clung together. In her mind she could hear his voice saying over and over, 'Come to bed, Edie—come to bed.' Tears filled her eyes and slid down her cheeks, and she felt their warm wetness slippery under his hand as his fingers caressed her face, and he raised it gently to his. She opened her eyes wide to stare into the silvery secrets of his, and everything she felt was there for him to see.

Her lips parted, whether to say I love you or just to receive his kiss she was never to know, for suddenly he broke the spell with a crude exclamation and abruptly put her from him.

He stooped to pick up her writing pad, then flung himself back in the chair where he had been sitting previously, completely ignoring her.

Edie stood with her head bowed, her body aching with unfulfilled hunger for him. She was only vaguely aware that he was reading her letter. She had too much else to contend with to care, and it seemed an eternity before she had gained enough control over her mind to tell herself she was glad he had let her go before she made a complete fool of herself. Her body and mind were in hopeless confusion. She wanted him but she didn't want him, she hated him but she loved him, and she discovered she was staring at him fixedly. Had he said Come to bed? or had she merely imagined it? One thing was for sure, though. He hadn't said I love you. And she had no way of knowing what his feelings were for Laurel Clarkson.

At that moment, he raised his head and looked at her.

'You've got a funny way of trying not to lose your head, Edie.'

'What?' she said stupidly.

He didn't repeat it. 'I haven't been helping you, of course. Believe it or not, I didn't mean to touch you tonight—not since you told me so plainly to lay off. I was sitting here drinking my Scotch and swearing I'd leave you alone. But I can't and that's basic, and it's time to lay our cards on the table. If what's upset you is the idea I've been fooling you—that I didn't really mean we'd think about taking our marriage seriously, and that's about what you say in your letter, isn't it?— then let's get that point cleared up for a start.' He put the writing pad on the table near his glass and looked into her eyes. 'Edie, will you marry me?'

Edie sank down into the chair behind her before her legs gave way. The colour drained from her face. 'You —you've had too much to drink,' she said shakily. 'We are married——'

He made an impatient gesture and his eyes smouldered across at her.

'Okay, I've had too much to drink. But not so much I don't know what I'm saying. The fact is, from almost the minute you and I have met, we've been juggling with our emotions. Despite the suggestion I made the other morning, I can't forget we're legally married—and I don't believe you can either. We're like two people who've fallen into the sea. It's no use trying to pretend we're still safely walking about on dry land. So I'll say it again—will you marry me?—for better or worse.'

'But you don't—we don't——' she stammered, unable to collect her senses.

'We don't what?'

'We don't—don't know each other. Not really.'

He looked at her through narrowed eyes. 'Is that what you really mean? Or are you trying to say we don't love each other—that love is in fact more than sexual attraction? I'm afraid just at this moment, I'm not capable of being metaphysical about it all ... Have you ever been in love, Edie?'

She moistened her lips, but instead of answering him she asked, 'Have you?'

He smiled crookedly. 'I'm thirty-five. It'd be odd if I hadn't been.' He lit a cigarette and offered it to her, then when she refused it, drew on it himself, frowningly. 'I've told you about Deborah. But that was a long time ago.'

'Yes, I know, but isn't there—someone else?' she asked. 'Laurel,' she wanted to say. 'Laurel Clarkson. You were engaged to her. Weren't you in love with her? Are you still in love with her?'

'Someone else?' he repeated. 'Now, you mean? For God's sake—what do you think? If there were someone else I'd hardly have got myself into this situation with you, would I? And I certainly wouldn't be asking you to marry me—again, and differently. I hope that answers your question. And now how about answering mine? Have you ever been in love?'

'Only with you,' she wanted to say, but he'd never

believe that. She said reluctantly, 'I suppose I've imagined I was in love.'

'Then try the real thing, Edie. Try falling in love with me, in fact. Stop fighting against nature and admit that the makings of love are there. Haven't you heard it said love's one of the pleasant end products of proximity? If that's so, then we've got it made—or just about. You can't get much closer than in bed together in the middle of the outback, I shouldn't imagine ... Now don't look at me like that. We've agreed I've had too much to drink and I'm not suggesting we start our new relationship within the next five minutes or so. I'll give you a day—two days—three, if you need them, to think the thing over. If your answer's no, then we'll have to part. We can't go on much longer the way things are—either of us.'

No, they couldn't—of course they couldn't, and Edie knew it. It was the old thing of playing with fire, and she was the one who was most likely to get burned. It made sense to sort it all out, once and for all, and of course she didn't want to go. She had a mad impulse to say, 'Yes, I'll marry you—I don't need time to think about it——' but before she could say it he had got to his feet.

'I'm going to take a walk, Edie, so I'll say goodnight now. You'll tell me during the next day or two what you've decided, won't you? In the meantime, perhaps you'd better not post that letter.'

In a moment he had gone, and even if he wasn't sober, his progress from the room was straight and steady. Edie sat staring ahead of her unseeingly for a full minute before, with a sigh, she tore the sheet from the pad, crumpled up her letter, and took herself off to bed.

CHAPTER NINE

DURING the night, she made up her mind recklessly but definitely that her answer was going to be yes. It couldn't possibly be anything else. To refuse him meant she would have to go, there was no argument about that. It was perfectly plain what was going to happen, and happen very soon, if she stayed, and she told herself she would forget about Laurel—he'd said there was no one else. Of course it would have been a great deal more reassuring if he'd said something casual such as, 'I was engaged to another girl recently, but we called it off'. It was the fact that he hadn't even mentioned Laurel that made her so uneasy.

Before she fell asleep she knew that even though he hadn't been quite sober—— 'No, let's face it,' she corrected herself wryly, he'd been definitely drunk—when he 'proposed' to her, she was going to tell him yes.

She had had vague ideas of rising early and getting it over and done with before Drew left the homestead for the muster camp, but although she woke early she didn't get up. She lay in bed listening to the faint sounds as he moved about the house—showering, dressing, getting his breakfast—and she made no move to go and find him. It was as if she were suddenly nervous of him. And anyhow, she excused herself, she didn't want to appear over-eager. Though that might appear just a little bit funny when you considered her—willingness in his arms.

'Tonight,' she thought, 'when we're in the sitting room after dinner. He'll ask me then if I've decided.'

Perhaps she'd tell him she had, or perhaps she'd say she hadn't quite made up her mind. It all depended how persuasive he was. Meanwhile, she wouldn't write to Barb. Not until it was all straightened out. It was crazy, really, when she came to think about it. She'd come racing up north to meet—and perhaps to marry—a complete stranger, with scarcely a qualm. And now that she'd actually fallen in love with him, she was almost sick with nerves at the idea of making the marriage real.

That morning as she told Ellen and Ruth what she wanted them to do in the house, she was aware she felt differently about it all. She was going to be the Missus here—the real Missus. This was going to be her house, her home. Her children would grow up here. This would be her kitchen—she could reorganise it as she chose without wondering if Mrs Wilson would mind.

She could hardly wait for the girls to go so that she could be on her own and take a long leisurely look around and decide on any alterations she was going to make. 'I'm going to live here—for always,' she kept reminding herself, and wondered why she felt deep down so unconvinced. Perhaps it was that little matter of love and romance. Did *he* believe that love was more than sexual attraction? And did he feel more than that for Edie Asher? Rather glumly, she admitted it was hardly likely. But surely it would work out somehow—it would have to. After all, she loved him—hopelessly, madly.

She was walking past Drew's office after the house girls had gone when she paused, and on impulse opened the door. All the packets and parcels that had been on the desk yesterday had gone. He'd have taken them out to the camp with him this morning—or over to the women in the bungalows, the women whom soon

she would have to get to know, now that she was really
going to belong here. The letters, too, had gone, all
excepting a small pile that must belong to Drew.

Edie moved further into the room. He'd said last
night he'd had a letter from his aunt, from Ireland—
to let him know what was happening on the other side
of the world. Almost without thinking, Edie picked
up the letters and thumbed quickly through them, looking for one with an Irish stamp. Laurel was in Ireland,
Mickie had said, so surely Drew's aunt would have
sent him news of her. The minute this thought entered
her head, Edie felt unbearably curious. Her fingers
began to tremble, and when she didn't find the letter
she wanted she felt both baffled and frustrated. She
flicked through the letters again. On most of them the
address was typewritten and Drew had scribbled something on an envelope here and there. Of course!—
they were all business letters. His aunt's was the only
personal mail he had received, so it would be somewhere else. Where?

After a second she opened the drawer of the desk—
guiltily, her heart beating fast. Incredibly it was there—
an envelope that bore a stamp marked Eire, with an in-
tricate Celtic design, no doubt from the Book of Kells.
It was postmarked Limerick, and as she held it in her
hand she fought a brief battle with herself as to whether
or not she should open it. It was despicable to read
someone else's personal mail—it was unforgivable. It
was the kind of thing one simply didn't do. Yet he'd
read the letter she'd written to Barb last night—even
though she hadn't wanted him to read it, hadn't given
him permission. It wasn't quite the same thing, of
course, but it was an approximation. His excuse had
been that he wanted to know what was going on in her

mind. Well, she wanted to know something too—something, anything—about Laurel.

She gave in to temptation and drew the folded pages from the envelope. She hated herself, despised herself, for doing it, but she did it all the same.

His aunt's handwriting was large and showy and quite easy to read, and her eyes skimmed over it with guilty speed. 'Dear Drew,' she read, 'I'm afraid I have some bad news for you. Laurel won't be coming back. In fact, by the time this letter reaches you, she'll be married to Greg. I'll admit I'm delighted, it's something I've always wanted, and I believe it would have happened years ago if you hadn't come between them. However, Laurel and Greg apart, I suppose the greatest blow to you will be losing the cattle station after all your determined efforts to commandeer it regardless of the rights of anyone else. I shouldn't need to remind you that Dhoora Dhoora was Greg's and my home for twelve years—and that I looked after Philip all that time. But for your influence, he would have married me, and that would have settled a number of things.

'However, it's all ending the way it should, thanks be, and I'll admit now that my motive in inviting Laurel to visit us was to give her a fair chance to decide who she really wanted, you or Greg—and incidentally, who's to have D.D., you or my son. Laurel loves it in Limerick as much as we do, and Greg will probably put D.D. up for sale and invest the money in the bloodstock farm we've acquired. One reason I'm telling you all this is to give you the opportunity of raising the money if you wish to buy the property. If you can't make it, or don't want to, I'm sure you'll be able to stay on as manager as it will probably be bought by one of the big pastoral companies ...'

Edie didn't read the rest. She had enough to digest

and she felt slightly sick as she folded the pages and put them back in the envelope. She put the letter carefully back in the desk, closed the drawer, and sank down into Drew's chair. She'd learned all she wanted and more. She knew now that Drew must have been hoping Laurel would come back to him. It had been outside his power to decide that, but he'd out-manoeuvred them all when it came to Dhoora Dhoora. Drew was clearly the winner there. Even if he were to lose the girl, he'd made sure that he'd keep the property. That was why he had married—temporarily—Alfreda Asher. Who, if Laurel were to come back, could quickly be dispensed with.

And Alfreda Asher now knew exactly why he had been drinking whisky last night. He had been drowning his sorrows. And he had asked her to marry him— in fact as well as in name—because he'd lost Laurel. While her heart ached for him, it ached for herself as well. She was still going to marry him even though she knew now that not one part of him belonged to her. No wonder he hadn't wanted to go into the metaphysics of love!

She cooked him a beautiful, exquisite dinner that night as if to help make up for what he had lost. Or was it to show him that he was getting quite a prize after all—a wife who could cook? Edie wasn't sure and she didn't care. She knew she was an idiot and she knew he didn't love her, and she knew most of all that she couldn't bear never to see him again.

Besides, in a way he needed her now. Wasn't that something?

He praised her for the meal, but it didn't give her much of a thrill. She discovered she felt constrained with him, knowing what she now knew, and it was a relief when he said he was going into the office—to catch up on some paper work, and to ring through to the outstation, or so he said.

'Oh, please give Mickie my love,' Edie said with a smile that she hoped didn't look as forced as it felt.

'I'll do that,' he agreed, and paused before leaving the room. 'By the way, I was talking to Frank Wilson today.'

'Oh. How is Mrs Wilson?'

'Fine—she's doing very nicely. Frank wanted to check up if it would be okay for her to spend two or three weeks with her sister over at the coast before she comes back.'

'That sounds a good idea,' Edie said cheerfully—and waited for him to ask her if she'd still be around. But he didn't. He smiled and continued on his way from the dining room.

Edie felt deflated. She'd have thought he'd want to know. It was as if last night had never happened, and she began to wonder if all those whiskies he'd drunk had made him say things he didn't remember. But most probably he simply wasn't in the mood for Edie. He was suffering still from the blow of knowing he'd lost Laurel irrevocably. Nothing she could say would make up for that, not even if she loved him a thousand times more than Laurel ever had.

She kept herself busy next day, working in the garden, so she'd be tired and maybe sleep well. The night was more or less a repetition of the previous one, with Drew doing a disappearing act so that once dinner was over she was on her own again. But this time, as he rose from the table, he said almost briskly, 'I'll want your answer tomorrow night, Edie. Three days is enough.'

Her heart thumped and she looked across at him as he stood behind his chair at the dining table. She was about to load some dishes on to a tray to take out to the kitchen and she put them down. Her lips parted, but on the point of telling him, 'I've decided now', she found she couldn't do it. Not—cold like that. Not while there was that guarded, closed look in his eyes. She needed some warmth—some—some come-on sign from him. Some encouragement, some enthusiasm, some indication that he wanted her to say yes. She wanted his touch, his kiss, his assurance of—of *something*, even though she couldn't expect assurance of love. In bed together in the middle of the outback, he'd said, love will come. But had he meant that she'd learn to love him? Or that they'd learn to love each other? 'Kiss me,' she implored him silently. 'Kiss me, so I can tell you yes.'

He said almost irritably as she stared at him dumbly, 'Well, what's the matter? You know what I'm talking about, don't you?'

She nodded and picked up the dishes again. 'Yes, of course, Drew. I promise I'll tell you tomorrow night.'

'You'd better,' he said coolly, and went on his way.

Next morning Edie dismissed Ruth and Ellen as soon as they'd done the dishes. She wanted to be by herself. She had some more thinking to do, because tonight she had to give Drew her answer and it was going to affect the rest of both their lives. It was going to be hard. She knew she was poor compensation for the loss of Laurel—not even second best, just someone who'd answered an ad. She'd have been a lot happier if she'd never read that letter, but accepted his assurance at its face value—that there was no one else. Sex can't take the place of love, she thought tiredly. Not even in the life of a man as strong and masculine as Drew. It was all very chastening and she felt herself of no account. Though she could give him her own love, she couldn't stir it in his heart. She could try, of course. She would have to try. If they were going on with the marriage it was no use taking a defeatist attitude.

With sudden determination she put on her sun hat and went into the garden to cut some roses—red roses, for the dinner table. When she brought them inside, she put them in a deep bowl of water in the laundry, away from the heat of the day. Then she went to her bedroom to decide what she'd wear for dinner—and for later, when she told him she'd marry him. Or at least, when she gave him permission to make love to her, she corrected herself wryly. She'd be romantic, she decided —she'd stir him up, quite deliberately. She chose a long flowered skirt, a creamy silk blouse with a plunging neckline; and she'd wear a red rose. She held the blouse up to herself and studied her reflection—her dark eyes, the dark swathe of hair falling over her shoulder—and another image came into her mind—blonde, laughing. Well, it was good they were so different. At least she'd never catch Drew looking at her and thinking he could see Laurel there.

Presently, barefooted for coolness and with one of Mrs Wilson's big aprons on over bra and briefs plus a cotton scarf tied over her hair, she did some dusting and polishing. She was in the kitchen, repapering some shelves, having removed the mixing bowls and other kitchen crockery they contained, when she became vaguely aware that she'd heard the sound of a car outside.

Was it Drew? Come back because he couldn't wait till tonight? Positively not because of that, but all the same the colour rushed to her cheeks and she thought in dismay of the scantiness of her clothing under the apron. There was no chance of making a dash for her bedroom, for already she heard footsteps and within seconds there was somebody in the doorway.

Edie stared. Her heart pounded and then seemed to stop. It had taken her only one shocked second to recognise Laurel Clarkson, and she stared and stared, like a rabbit hypnotised by a snake. Laurel stared back at her. Her eyes were blue and a little hard, her fair hair was beautiful, immaculate under its shimmer of lacquer. She wore a khaki-coloured skirt and blouse in a soft uncrushable cotton mixture, and the heels of her shoes were slim and high. Edie felt exactly as if she were seeing a ghost. She moved two paces to rest her back against the edge of the sink, newly conscious of what she was wearing.

Laurel's eyes moved to look her over rapidly and then, in a voice as chilling as her glance, she exclaimed, 'Who on earth are you? You can't possibly be the new boreman's wife!'

'No. I—Mrs Wilson was taken to hospital with appendicitis,' Edie got out huskily. 'She won't be back for a few weeks—she's going to convalesce at the coast.'

'And you've taken over the housekeeping?' Laurel said. Edie definitely didn't like her cynical smile or the scepticism in her voice. 'Well, well—how did you come to be chosen for the job, I wonder?'

Edie looked at her helplessly. Surely she must be dreaming—or having hallucinations or something. Laurel couldn't be here, in the kitchen at Dhoora Dhoora. She was far away in Ireland—she was married to Greg Sutton. A sudden thought struck her. Perhaps Greg was here too! Ignoring the other girl's unpleasant insinuations, she asked tentatively, 'Is your husband with you?'

'My husband?' Laurel looked surprised. 'I don't happen to have a husband yet. I'm Drew Sutton's fiancée—I've been in Ireland for a holiday ... Who *are* you, when you get out of your apron and mob cap, anyhow?'

'I—I——' Edie stopped. A wave of nausea engulfed her as the implications of what was happening came home to her. Drew's aunt had been wrong. Her efforts to part Drew and Laurel hadn't succeeded after all. Laurel wasn't married to Greg and never intended to be. She'd come back to Drew—and now of course he'd want Edie out of the way, their marriage annulled as he'd planned in the beginning. But he'd never let them know about his marriage, in Ireland. Would he want Edie to break the news? Wasn't it better to let him do it himself—in his own way? Thank heavens, she thought incoherently, their marriage hadn't been consummated—not yet. If Laurel had come back just a little later—tomorrow even—it might have been very different. For Edie, that was.

'Well?' said Laurel Clarkson. She had marched right into the kitchen and she was looking about her almost as if she expected to find evidence of—of immorality, Edie thought on the verge of hysterical laughter, though she was not really even the tiniest bit amused. Laurel whirled around suddenly and stood not more than a foot away. 'Who the hell are you?'

Edie struggled to regain her self-possession. After all, she had done nothing, to be spoken to in this angry contemptuous way, as though she were some little tramp who had moved in with Laurel's fiancé. The real facts were very different, and yet she couldn't say baldly, 'I'm Drew's wife'. It was a statement that required a terrific lot of qualifying, and after a momentary hesitation she said quietly and with dignity, 'I think Drew had better explain the situation to you, Miss Clarkson.'

The other girl glared at her haughtily. '*Drew?* Don't

you mean Mr Sutton? And are you by any chance trying to give me the impression that there's something
between you and my fiancé?' Her eyes raked over Edie
and now for the first time she seemed to register that
she was wearing next to nothing under the big apron.
'Exactly where is Mr Sutton right now?' she snapped
out.

'He's out at the muster camp,' said Edie, her head
up though inwardly she was in danger of going to
pieces. This was a nightmare—and she just didn't like
Laurel Clarkson at all, despite her pretty face.

'By the look of you, you're doing your level best to
get him into bed with you,' Laurel commented. 'Have
you succeeded?'

A spot of colour came into Edie's pale cheeks. 'Perhaps you'd better ask him about that, too.'

'I shan't bother—I can guess,' the other girl bit out.
'But I promise you here and now that you've spent your
last day—and your last night—in this house ... Which
paddock is being mustered?'

'I'm afraid I have no idea,' Edie said coolly. 'You
might be able to find out from Harry.'

'I can find out without Harry's help,' Laurel snorted.
'Drew keeps track of the camps on the chart in his
office. But I suppose you wouldn't have the intelligence
to know that. You'd better get this mess cleared up,'
she added, indicating the things Edie had taken from
the shelves. 'You won't be staying here now I'm back.'

She turned on her heel and marched off, and Edie
stayed where she was, feeling shattered, indignant, and
singularly helpless. How good it would have been to
put that rude, arrogant girl in her place—to tell her,
'I'm Drew Sutton's wife'. Suddenly her eyes filled with
tears, and she turned and began blindly putting the
crockery back on the shelves. Not because Laurel had

told her to do so, but because it was an inescapable fact that this was Laurel's kitchen now. At that moment, Edie knew exactly how much she had wanted it to be hers. And she knew that secretly, deep in her heart, she had believed there'd be a happy ending for her and Drew. But there wouldn't be. The happy ending was for Drew and Laurel. Drew wouldn't want her around any more than Laurel did—and she wouldn't want to be around.

He'd be stunned when Laurel turned up at the muster camp, she thought—stunned and ecstatic. He'd explain away his marriage to Edie without any trouble at all. He knew he could trust her not to make mischief —nor to tell Laurel anything she ought not to know, such as that he'd asked Edie only the other night to marry him—to really marry him. So why was she hiding the basic facts from Laurel now? Didn't that make it look as though there *were* something to hide? What a fool she'd been! By far the best thing to have done would have been to tell Laurel—simply and coolly and impersonally—the truth, as it had been back in the beginning when Drew had explained so clearly that he wanted a marriage certificate but not a wife.

'I'll tell her,' Edie thought, and hurried into the hall-way immediately. But she was just in time to see Laurel, still in her smart khaki outfit, disappearing down the front steps in the direction of the car parked out there. Apparently she'd discovered to her satisfaction where the muster camp was, and as Edie watched, she started up the motor and drove off, the wheels of her car kicking up a spurt of gravel as she accelerated.

Well, her chance at honesty was gone now, and she wasn't really sorry. She couldn't pretend she fancied another encounter with Drew's fiancée.

They'd be home later on—both of them, she thought

as she stood disconsolately at the front door. She thought sadly of the dinner she had planned, the roses she had cut, of her little schemes for using her femininity to beguile, to stir, Drew. And there was an intolerable ache in her heart. She didn't want to be here when they came back—she dreaded the thought of an evening with Drew and Laurel. How could they possibly —any of them—act civilised in such a situation? Laurel hadn't been particularly civilised already.

'No,' Edie thought wretchedly, 'I can't cook dinner for them as though everything were fine and dandy. I can't smile and talk and pretend. I love him—I want him—I wish I were dead!'

But wishing yourself dead was a defeatist attitude, and Edie simply wasn't a defeatist. She decided to take a shower, wash her hair, dress herself in something cool and pretty and cheerful. She'd make herself a salad and an icy cold fruit drink, and she'd take off her wedding ring and be plain Edie Asher again in every way. She reminded herself with a rather desperate optimism that it could have been worse—much, much worse. She and Drew could have been lovers by now—she could have told him yes last night. Thank heavens she hadn't! Now she could pretend that her answer was going to be no. It would make her feel better—and him too, she hoped.

She told herself this over and over again later, as she picked at her salad on the verandah. It was after two o'clock, but she wasn't hungry, she was too uptight at the thought of the evening ahead of her—of seeing Drew again. With Laurel, the girl he loved. It was going to be plain hell, and though she knew she should be happy for him, she just wasn't that noble. She hated Laurel. The best she could hope for was that Drew would be merciful enough to arrange for her to leave tomorrow, somehow or other. It was a pity she couldn't disappear this minute, by some magic means or other. But unfortunately she didn't have a fairy godmother to grant her wishes.

Edie abandoned her salad, finished her orange drink, and carried her plate and glass inside. She had almost reached the kitchen when she heard the sound of a car and her heart gave a leap. Laurel—or Drew—or both of them already! Oh God! Well, at least she was dressed and in her right mind, and at least she'd decided what line she'd take. But she knew very well it was going to be an ordeal, and rather than hasten its beginning, she continued on her way to the kitchen.

Someone knocked on the front door as she rinsed her glass and plate at the sink. What on earth was that in aid of? she wondered, frowning. To let her know they were there? More knocking—louder this time—and an aggressive male voice called out, 'Is anyone at home?'

The colour fled from Edie's face. That voice! It was Joe!

A moment later she discovered him standing on the verandah looking down the hallway. It was so unexpected, she hardly knew what to think, and even while her heart sank at this new complication an inner voice told her mockingly, 'Maybe you have a fairy godmother after all! Maybe this is your chance to escape the trauma of an evening alone with Laurel and Drew.'

'Joe!' she heard herself greeting him, her voice falsely bright. 'Where on earth did you come from? Come along inside——' She looked at him curiously as he accepted her invitation. He looked so slim, so much smaller than she remembered him. But that was because Drew was—— 'How did you get here?' she asked vivaciously.

'I flew up to Narrunga and hired a car,' he said. He

went ahead of her into the sitting room, and before
he sat down he looked about him, narrow-eyed, in the
same suspicious way Laurel had looked around the
kitchen earlier, Edie thought, wryly amused.

'You came all this way to see me!' she exclaimed,
knowing she sounded affected. 'Sit down, Joe! Would
you like a drink?—a beer—some tea——'

'I'll have a beer, thanks, if you've got it,' he said,
sounding slightly puzzled. 'Isn't there anyone else
around here?'

'Not at the moment,' she admitted. 'Just make yourself comfortable and I'll get some beer from the fridge.
I'll be right back.'

A number of thoughts jostled around in her mind
as she left him and went back to the kitchen. Obviously,
Barb had told him where she was, and obviously she
could make some use of him. Couldn't she—couldn't
she have her wish and simply have disappeared before
Drew and Laurel came back? Wouldn't that be better
—far better—than asking Joe to stay the night? Of
course it would, yet she baulked at it. However painful
it was, she knew she longed to see Drew again, under
any circumstances. She knew too that if she could avoid
it then she wasn't going to allow herself to see him. She
must persuade Joe to drive her to Narrunga this afternoon. Once a thing is over, it's over, she told herself, as
she took a couple of cans of beer from the refrigerator.
It was something she'd learned in hospital when a
patient died. You could make yourself into a mental
case if you wept and worried and churned it over and
over in your mind. She was going to have to learn to
forget Drew, and the time to start was now.

When she went back into the sitting room, Joe asked
her abruptly, 'What's going on here, Edie?'

Stupidly, she was caught unaware. She'd been too

busy with her immediate problems to wonder what she was going to tell Joe. The fact was, she wasn't greatly concerned what he thought. He meant nothing to her—nothing at all, though possibly he didn't realise that yet.

She sat down and told him blandly, 'Nothing's been going on here. I don't know what you're talking about.'

His eyes were blue and friendly, but just now there was mistrust in them as they moved thoughtfully over Edie—her shining dark hair, her pale face and shadowed eyes, her pretty tomato red dress, her bare brown legs and high-heeled sandals.

'Don't give us that stuff, Edie,' he said after a moment. 'Barb finally opened up and told me exactly what you'd been up to—coming up here to marry some bushie you'd never set eyes on. I suppose that was my fault in a way. Will you believe me when I tell you I'm sorry I made myself so objectionable that night—the last time we met? I haven't been able to get you off my mind, you know. In fact I——'

Edie interrupted quickly, afraid he was going to say he loved her or wanted her to marry him or something. 'It wasn't your fault at all, Joe—forget it.'

He frowned slightly and she thought in an impersonal way, 'He's quite nice really—I can see why I thought I was in love with him.'

'Anyhow,' he went on, 'I had to come and find you. Barb really had the wind up. All she'd heard from you was that you weren't being rushed to the altar and you were going to spend a few days on a cattle station—she showed me your letter. After that, absolutely nothing. What were we to think? You might have been dead!'

'Oh dear,' Edie said inadequately. 'I knew she was a little bit worried—I had a letter the other day. But I had no idea it was as bad as that.'

'Well, it was,' Joe said grimly. 'And since she hadn't a clue what to do about it, I offered to come and investigate. For all we knew, you could have been in the clutches of a sadist, or something—unable to get away. Instead of which, what do I find? You come floating to the door—come on in, Joe, have a beer, all that stuff.' He gave her a straight look, drank down the rest of his beer and as he reached for another can he asked her flatly, 'So what has been happening?'

Edie smiled uneasily. She didn't feel like telling Joe the whole story. It really wasn't any business of his that she'd made a marriage contract with a stranger, fallen in love with him, and now wanted to get out because his ex-fiancée had come back into his life.

'I'm sorry I worried you by not writing,' she said after a second. 'But as you can see, I haven't been locked up by a sadist or anything like that. All the same, I'm glad you've come, Joe. I'd rather like to go home. Today,' she added, and finished with an appealing smile, 'As soon as you've finished your beer, in fact.'

He stared at her, forgetting the can in his hands. 'What? Leave now—straight away? Just like that? You mean you *haven't* been able to get away—you've been a kind of prisoner here! What's this bloke been doing to you? By God, I'd like to push his face in!'

Edie bit her lip. The thought of Joe pushing Drew's face in was quite ludicrous. It was far more likely to happen the other way around if Joe insisted on a fight. She said hastily, 'Please don't get worked up about nothing, Joe. Of course I haven't been kept a prisoner. It's just that I've—I've been here long enough now, and it would be convenient to go with you instead of having to mess around making other arrangements. Drew won't mind.'

'Won't he? Why not?' Joe asked aggressively. 'Barb

said he wanted a wife. So what's wrong with you?' As if struck by a sudden thought he glanced at her left hand, and she was thankful she'd discarded her ring.

She shrugged slightly, though she'd paled. 'Nothing. He does want a wife, but it's—it's not going to be me, it's going to be someone else.'

'Good God! You mean he's had other girls here? What kind of a man is he?'

'Oh, leave it alone,' Edie said shortly. 'Don't let your imagination run away with you. I told you nothing's been going on and I mean it. Now if you'll excuse me, I'll——'

'You're going to see this guy—tell him you're leaving? I'll come with you,' said Joe, jumping to his feet. 'If he tries to throw his weight around, stop you from leaving, I'll knock him flat!'

'Oh, sit down, Joe,' Edie sighed. 'I'm not going to see him—I'll leave a note. He's miles and miles away at the muster camp, I don't even know which direction. I was merely going to say I'll pack my things.' She got up from her chair. 'It won't take me long. If you want the bathroom there's one at the end of the side verandah. And if you want another beer you can find the kitchen and get what you what from the fridge.'

But Joe didn't want the bathroom and he didn't want another beer. He followed Edie to her room, looked suspiciously at the double bed, then leaned against the wall and watched her as she packed her clothes. She wanted to weep a little by now, and she wished he'd go away, but as he didn't, she could only try to hide the fact that her mouth was trembling and her eyes were full of tears.

'It's the weirdest thing I've heard,' he commented, as she took an armful of clothes from the wardrobe and began folding them carelessly and laying them in her suitcase any old how. 'Advertising for a wife and then—— How many girls have there been here, for God's sake? And where are they all now?'

Edie laughed a little shrilly and brushed a tear away. 'For goodness' sake, Joe, what are you trying to make out of this? There's just me and this girl he's going to marry. Laurel,' she said, and her voice broke. She bundled a pile of underthings from the drawer, stuffed them in her suitcase and snapped the lid shut.

'You're not telling me the truth, are you?' demanded Joe. 'There's more in this than you're admitting to. I'd like to know——'

Edie's nerves gave way. 'I've told you all you need to know,' she snapped. 'And none of it's any of your business anyhow. Isn't it enough you've found me safe and sound and I'm coming back to Sydney? Now please go away and let me write my—my thank-you note so we can get to Narrunga before dark.'

Joe gave her a hostile look, and for a moment she wondered if he'd refuse to take her. But he wasn't as mean as that. 'All right,' he shrugged, 'if you're in such a hurry. But in my opinion something should be done about people like this kinky cattleman.' He picked up her suitcase. 'I'll take this out to the car. You scribble off your note—though I don't know what you're thanking him for.'

Edie was quivering. She could have flung herself down on the bed and howled. Instead she reached for her writing pad and ballpoint. Maybe it was as well she had to write her farewell note to Drew in such a hurry. This way, the agony wouldn't be so long-drawn-out.

'Dear Drew,' she wrote, and continued with barely a pause. 'I know you'll be surprised, but this is to say goodbye and thanks. Joe turned up this afternoon by a stroke of good luck, and he's taking me to Narrunga to catch the plane home. I didn't plan to stay much longer anyhow. I'm so glad for you that Laurel's come back. Let's hope it won't take too long to have our marriage annulled. I wish you every happiness. Alfreda Asher.'

She read it through quickly and decided she'd done well. It was innocuous enough for even Laurel to read, but all the same she had to dash the tears from her eyes before she wrote Drew's name on an envelope and put the folded sheet inside. She left it in his bedroom—propped up against the pillow so he would be sure not to miss it when he came home. And so he would get it before Laurel saw it—she hoped.

Then she hurried out to the car.

CHAPTER TEN

ONCE they'd left the main gate of Dhoora Dhoora behind them Joe wanted to talk. Edie didn't. She felt exhausted—as though she'd been put through an emotional mangle. Coming away with Joe like this without seeing Drew, knowing she'd never see him again, not ever—it reminded her of when, as a child, she'd got on to one of those long and terrifying slippery dips at a fun-fair. The moment she'd taken off she'd wished herself back at the top—but there was no going back, just as there seemed to be no going back now. She had to ride it out to the end.

But Joe's incessant questioning, his determination to

find something sensational, nasty, unsavoury, about Drew and the set-up at Dhoora Dhoora—about what she'd been through—annoyed her beyond endurance.

'You can tell me, Edie—I won't be shocked—nothing shocks me. And it will do you good to get it out of your system. You look like you've had more than enough of whatever it is, anyhow.'

'I've had more than enough of you needling me, Joe,' Edie said edgily. 'All I want is for you to be quiet.' She sounded disagreeable and she felt disagreeable, and she knew Joe's feelings were hurt, but after that he did keep quiet. For a short while she felt guilty and she even considered telling him the truth. But it was all so complicated, and she was quite likely to break down in the middle of it.

After a while, she closed her eyes. She felt a couple of weak tears run down her cheeks and she wished the time would pass—weeks and weeks of it, months and months and years of it, just so that this bad moment and all the unbearable moments ahead would be behind her and lost for ever. Once she heard a car whizz past scattering gravel and Joe muttered something about women drivers.

Perhaps another ten minutes went by, and then Edie's eyes flew open as she felt the car swerve violently across the gravel road and bump along over the stiff clumps of grasses on the verge.

'What's happened?' she gasped out.

Joe pulled on the wheel, braked, and stopped with a final jerk that jarred her spine, his side of the car narrowly missing the post and wire fence.

'Some lunatic's trying to run me off the road!' he snapped furiously, turning his head towards a Land Rover that had pulled up at an angle to his car. 'Get out of the way, Edie—let me out!' he exclaimed.

Edie scarcely heard him. She had seen that the driver of the Land Rover was Drew Sutton and her heart began to beat double fast. For a moment she thought she was going to faint. Unaware of her pale face Joe, who couldn't get out by his own door, jammed as it was against the fence, leaned across and opened the door on her side and in a moment the two of them were out of the car.

Drew too had left his vehicle and came round the bonnet towards them. He looked purposeful, his face was streaked with red dust, he wore a black handkerchief at the neck of his checked shirt. His sleeves were rolled up above the elbows and his boots and his narrow-legged black pants were dusty. He looked rough and tough and his silver-grey eyes glinted like ice against the darkness of his skin as they went from Edie to Joe and back again—slowly, assessingly.

'What the hell were you doing?' demanded Joe, his voice hoarse and croaky as Drew came nearer—almost as if he were scared. Edie had a weak desire to giggle. Perhaps he thought this was some kind of outback bandit come to kill him or to take his money—or his girl. He was possibly thinking it would have been more strategic to stay in the car now, and he actually grabbed hold of Edie and thrust her behind.

'You're Joe, I take it,' Drew said with an odd kind of formality. 'I'm Drew Sutton from Dhoora Dhoora.'

Edie saw Joe's shoulders move in a breath of relief and then he stiffened. She remembered him saying he'd like to smash Drew's face in, but he didn't attempt that. He said aggressively, 'So what? Does that give you the right to run my car off the road? If you think you're going to stop me taking Edie back to Sydney, then you can damn well think again. She's not going back to Dhoora Dhoora—she doesn't want to.'

'Relax,' Drew drawled. 'I don't want to do anything Edie doesn't want.' He sounded polite, but the smile that showed the whiteness of his teeth looked somehow cruel in his dust-stained face. Edie found she couldn't keep her eyes off him. 'All I want is to ask Edie a question. Nothing more than that.'

He was looking at her now—straight and hard and searchingly, right into her eyes, and she felt herself quivering, melting, dying of her need for him.

What was the question he wanted to ask her? The top of her mind told her it was going to be something about the annulment of their marriage, but the expression in his eyes told her it was nothing so remote, nothing so cold.

'Edie's not interested in your questions,' Joe blustered. 'She's finished with involving herself in your crackpot schemes ... Get your car out of my way. We want to go.'

Drew's nostrils whitened slightly, but otherwise he showed no sign of emotion. 'I'm sorry, but I have to ask you to wait. And I'll make it two questions now. You can listen if you must, though it's a very personal matter ... Edie, tell me this. Did you, at some time or other, ask this—friend of yours to come and fetch you?'

Edie shook her head, wishing she didn't feel so weak at the knees. It was just—just seeing him again. It did something drastic to her.

'No? I didn't think so. And the other question—the important one. Did Laurel's arrival make you change your mind about what you were going to tell me to-night?'

'I—I don't know what you mean,' she lied, her cheeks flushing scarlet, then paling. 'Didn't you get my letter? I explained——'

'Of course I got your letter. That's how I knew where to find you.' His eyes searched her own. It was a ridiculous situation, looking at each other, talking to each other as if Joe were simply not there, while he stayed doggedly in front of Edie as though protecting her from something. 'Edie, for God's sake, don't pretend you don't know what I mean. I've waited patiently for your answer for three days—my God, I've been patient! Then you just write me a letter and walk out. I don't know what Laurel told you, but I can guess. I only hope you didn't believe it.'

'Write you a letter and walk out!' Edie echoed, only half aware of what he'd said after that. 'What did you expect me to do, I'd like to know? Make a—a threesome tonight?'

Joe moved. 'Come on, Edie. Whatever it is you've got yourself into you're better out of it.' He turned and grasped her arm, but she pulled away from him.

'It won't be a threesome,' said Drew, still ignoring Joe. 'Laurel's gone.' Now it was he who took hold of her arm and he did it roughly, possessively, pulling her towards him with a sharp movement. She didn't resist, and she was so close to him she felt herself melting, giving way, wanting him.

'Where's she gone?' she asked huskily.

'I don't know and I don't care. Come home, Edie——'

It was the way he said it. It was like when he said, Come to bed. She said weakly, 'Oh, Drew——' and leaned her head against his chest.

'*Yes?*' Drew muttered against her hair.

'Yes,' she breathed. 'Oh—yes!' She didn't understand—not yet. But she would. She only knew it was going to come right after all.

After that, she was rather vague as to what happened.

She remembered leaning out of the Land Rover and calling across to Joe, as they took off, 'Tell Barb it's all right. Truly. I'll be in touch.'

And then she and Drew were alone.

She knew she was utterly committed now, and while something in her was at peace there were things she had to know. About Laurel. She had gone, but Edie didn't know why. Reason told her it was because Drew wanted it that way. Hadn't he said, 'I don't care where she's gone?' And hadn't he—hadn't he held Edie in his arms and said 'Come home'—in a way that destroyed all her defences?

'Drew——' she began uncertainly.

He was driving fast—dangerously fast except that there were no other cars on the road. All that was following them was a cloud of red dust.

'What?' he cast her a quick, half-smiling glance. 'Have you suddenly remembered your baggage? Don't worry—I didn't forget it, it's stashed away in the back. You won't have to go naked.'

'Oh,' she said vaguely. 'No, I—I wasn't thinking about my clothes, Drew. I was—I was wondering about Laurel.'

He swore softly beneath his breath. 'Damn Laurel ... Well, I suppose we must talk about her some time, so let's get it over. What's on your mind?'

What was on her mind! What an infuriating male attitude to take! Her jealousy was dying hard, but to be fair, she realised he didn't know much about that. She said mildly, 'I'm sorry, Drew, but if you don't tell me I'll always be wondering. I knew you were engaged to her, you see—long before she told me so today.'

'You did? How?'

'Oh, I found out accidentally. There was that room at Dhoora Dhoora and then—well, Mickie thought you'd told me from something I said and——'

'Good God!' he interrupted. 'Was that what got into you the day we were at the outstation? Why on earth didn't you tell me?'

'Why didn't *you* tell *me*?' she countered. 'You could have—right at the beginning, when you explained why you needed a wife.'

'I could see no reason to bring Laurel into it. The engagement was off, and all I was planning, if you can remember that far back, was a temporary alliance with a girl I had no intention of becoming involved with. I certainly didn't know I was going to fall in love with you then, Edie.'

Her heart missed a beat. 'When *did* you fall in love with me, Drew?'

He stepped a little harder on the accelerator. 'For heaven's sake don't let's start talking about that sort of thing now,' he said half humorously. 'I know where it will lead to even if you don't—and surely by now you know my preference for making love in bed.'

Her pulses stirred and the colour came into her cheeks. Her thoughts raced ahead to when they'd be at the homestead—alone, and—well, she'd said yes now, hadn't she? Somehow she didn't think the dinner she'd planned—or even the roses—would be put on the table till very very late tonight, if at all ... With an effort she came back to the present.

'What I was doing in contracting that marriage,' said Drew, 'was making a counter-move to defeat my aunt's strategies. But I suppose that doesn't make a lot of sense to you.' Actually, it made more sense than he knew, because she'd read his aunt's letter, but she wasn't going to confess to that now. 'You know about my cousin Greg,' Drew continued. 'Of course my aunt wanted him to take over Dhoora Dhoora, and for that reason she didn't want Laurel to marry me. I think I told you once she has a great head for strategy——'

'So she invited Laurel to Ireland,' Edie put in.

'Right. After having first prepared the ground by giving Laurel the idea she was something of a *femme fatale* and could take her pick between me and Greg—thereby, of course, deciding who was to have Dhoora Dhoora. It's wonderful how a sense of power can go to a woman's head. Laurel fell for the deal because at one stage she and Greg had had quite an affair—until she'd decided she'd set her cap at me. Anyhow, I was well aware of my aunt's motives, and I told Laurel that she could choose between me and a trip to Ireland. In effect, if she went, then we were washed up.'

'And she—went?' Edie asked.

'Yes, she went. I didn't tell her my own plans, of course. She decided she didn't like being dictated to, and the way she saw it was that I was going to need a wife very soon—so I was in no position to dictate. She thought she could come back if it pleased her.'

'Didn't she—love you?'

He grimaced. 'Let's face it, it wasn't exactly a love match on either side. I'd never fallen in love since Debbie died, and it looked as if I never would. I had to have a wife, and Laurel was willing, so——' He shrugged. 'It didn't matter to me that Laurel loved herself better than anyone. She's not warm like you, Edie—she's selfish and cerebral and she liked her feeling of power, not knowing how ill-based it was. Oh, I daresay she thought Ireland might have more to offer her than the outback, and no doubt there was the thought that if Greg sold Dhoora Dhoora there'd be all that money to play around with.'

'But she came back—she chose you, Drew,' said

Edie, well aware that his aunt, in her letter, had said Laurel was going to marry Greg.

'Oh yes, she chose me,' Drew said cynically. 'She didn't tell me why, but my guess is she somehow or other discovered she wasn't going to have much say in what was to be done with the money.'

At that point their conversation came to a temporary standstill, because they'd reached Dhoora Dhoora and Edie had to start opening gates and closing them again.

They didn't talk again, in fact, till they were home, and Drew had carried her luggage back into the bedroom she'd left with such different feelings earlier in the afternoon—in what seemed another lifetime.

He set her suitcase down and looked across at her as she stood near the bed, and his eyes explored the whole of her as he said slowly, 'Remember the first time you came here, Edie—before we were married?'

Edie nodded. If she wanted, she thought, she could have gone over every minute of her life—in detail—from the first minute she met Drew. He had changed it so drastically. She remembered the night she'd told him she didn't want him coming into her room, and she remembered that evening in the rose garden when he'd kissed her for the first time. More than kissed her. He'd just come home from the muster camp and his face and his clothes had been covered in red dust just as they were now. She'd told him scornfully that she didn't find him attractive, yet deep down, even then, she'd known that wasn't true. Even then she'd found him madly exciting, and she knew she'd never been the same after that kiss.

'It's turned out unexpectedly, hasn't it?' Drew said reminiscently into her thoughts. He'd come across the room to her and now he raised his hand and drew one dust-roughened finger slowly down the smooth curve of her cheek. His eyes were more serious than she had ever seen them, and they stared at each other for a long moment while his finger caressed her cheek, then moved to her throat. Edie wanted to cry, simply because he was there and she was looking into his eyes— loving him. It had had to come right: she knew that now. They must have been meant by the gods to meet —it couldn't possibly have worked out as it had otherwise.

'When I brought you home that day,' Drew told her, 'I didn't have the slightest idea I was going to fall so damn hard in love with you—even though your looks nearly knocked me out. All I knew at the beginning was that I badly wanted to make love to you. And I was so entirely ignorant of your character I took it for granted you'd slept with other men. Do you know— the fact you hadn't really shook me? It was round about then I began to realise how irrevocably I'd fallen in love with you.'

'I—I wish you'd told me about Laurel then,' said Edie.

His lips curved in a crooked smile. 'Good God! I had enough to contend with without tossing in the irrelevant details of an engagement that had ended without a tinge of regret on my part. I'm aware a woman's imagination can really run riot over something like that.'

'Mine did,' Edie admitted, though it didn't seem to matter now. 'I hated you and I hated Laurel. I guess I even hated myself. And when—when she came back today and said she was going to marry you, I think I just wanted to die.'

'You make me feel a brute,' he muttered. He touched his lips to her eyelids, and then his arms went around her and he pulled her down on the bed with him. All her longing for him was stirred up as he held her against him and kissed her hungrily.

'I love you, Edie,' he said a minute later, his voice low and urgent.

'I love you too, Drew—so much it hurts.' Her lips found his this time and he moved away from her.

'Don't,' he said. He let go of her and sat up. 'Don't make love to me that way, Edie—not yet. I'm filthy. I can't go to bed with you like this—not your first time. Can you wait while I shower?'

'If you really want me to,' she said huskily. 'But I— I don't care if you're showered or not, Drew—I love you.' Her hands reached for him and moved to the muscles of his chest under his shirt.

'Stop it, Edie,' he groaned, coming down to her again. 'Oh God—I'm glad no one else has ever made love to you! I think I'd want to kill him. Old-fashioned, aren't I?'

Edie didn't care if he was old-fashioned or not. His mouth was against hers and then he was saying the words she most wanted to hear.

'Come to bed, Edie—come to bed.'

Celebrate Harlequin's 30th Anniversary...

...with this special anniversary book!

The first 30 years of the world's best romance fiction

This invaluable guide to your romance reading contains:

- numerical and alphabetical listings of Harlequin titles
- heartwarming glimpses into the lives of many of your favorite authors as they tell their own stories
- photographs of some of these authors
- a fascinating look at the origins of the Harlequin emblem
- 4 pages of beautiful color photographs showing some of your favorite books— old and new
- delightful photographs of book covers through the years

The first 30 years of the world's most popular romance fiction

This exciting 292-page volume contains a complete history of our publishing program—from 1949 to 1979.

Don't miss this beautifully designed anniversary book. A must for every Harlequin reader!

Only $1.25

Complete and mail this coupon today!

JOY ROMANCE LOVE

Harlequin Omnibus

THREE love stories in ONE beautiful volume

The joys of being in love...
the wonder of romance...
the happiness that true love brings...

Harlequin Presents...

The beauty of true romance...
The excitement of world travel...
The splendor of first love...